COVE HARBOR COMEUPPANCE

COVE HARBOR COMEUPPANCE

A SHORT MYSTERY COLLECTION

VOLUME I

ANNA DUNWORTH

© AD Writing LLC (2025)

www.annadunworth.com

ISBN: 979-8-9922497-1-2

Content warnings are available at
www.annadunworth.com/content-warnings

This is a work of fiction. All characters, organizations, events, and settings are products of the author's imagination or used fictitiously.

for my hometown

COVE HARBOR COMEUPPANCE
VOLUME I

Murder in the Marina

Who killed Gary Jones?

The body of a local Cove Harbor fisherman is discovered on the docks early one September morning. Who killed Gary Jones? Or better yet, who will miss him?

A Holiday Homicide

Who killed Mindy Pringle?

The holiday season takes a perilous turn when the wife of a local philanthropist collapses in the coffee shop. How did she die? And who is behind it?

Murder in the Main Office

Who killed Principal Kirk?

One rainy spring day at Cove Harbor High, the principal is found murdered in the Main Office. Many held a grudge against him, but who hated him enough to kill?

A Memorial Day Murder

Who killed Frankie Fenton?

The conductor of the Cove Harbor Community Band falls dead at the Memorial Day Parade. With a band director this dodgy, it won't be easy finding someone without a motive.

A Shot in the Crowd

Who killed Mayor Clark?

The mayor is shot to death during an impromptu press conference on a sunny afternoon. Who could want the leader of this small town to perish? And why?

"As one makes one's bed, so one finds it."

French Proverb

MURDER IN THE MARINA

A BODY ON THE DOCKS

September 17
5:13 AM

Wings battered the quiet morning as the seagulls hurled themselves into the air, screeching nearly as loudly as the young woman who startled them into flight. They soared above her abandoned paintbrushes, now scattered along the docks, some slipping through the planks into the marina beneath.

A bottle popped open, oozing steadily into something infinitely more sinister.

The amateur artist clutched her face as her paint melded into the congealing blood of a fisherman sprawled ahead. The bright red-orange, carefully selected in imitation of the morning sun, now sunk into the aged wood, forever staining the scene in her memory.

Though she didn't notice in her haste, the mixture trailed

horribly to a bracelet of freshwater pearls with a single stone, catching the sunrise to glow redder than the dawning sky above. It glittered there, a sliver of delicate luxury amidst the carnage.

She ran, letting her small canvas bounce carelessly along the pier, flying up the small ladder to the grassy park at street level. She tore across the green, clearing the roughly paved road in seconds, jumping lightly over a fallen gold car magnet along the way.

All the while, her shouts rang through the sleepy village, unrelenting until she reached the police station. She pounded violently on the door, shaking the locked handles, until a frazzled Cove Harbor cop let her inside. There, she would tell the officers of her discovery, kicking off their first murder investigation in nearly three decades.

A short walk away, Gary Jones lay face down on the docks, his last breath having left him hours earlier. Blood sat thick and still around the violent stab wounds across his back, inches below his disheveled hair, unkempt and matted from a night on the salty marina.

Who killed Gary Jones? Or maybe it would be better to ask who would miss him. His family? His oldest friends? The fish he pursued in the nearby waters or the wealthy tourists he encountered each summer? One thing is certain - Gary Jones will never walk the streets of this little seaside town again.

LINDA JONES

September 16
7:02 AM

"Enough!" Linda shouted. "I said you can't go, and I meant it. This conversation is over!"

Sarah roared in frustration before seizing her torn backpack from the kitchen counter. She flung it over her shoulder and glared turned back to her mother, eyes darkened in a gaze to kill.

"You're so unfair! I bet Dad would let me go! He knows how important this trip is to me, and it's probably the only chance I'll EVER have to see Paris! Not to mention that I'll be the ONLY one in French class who doesn't get to go!"

Sarah stomped through the kitchen and out the front door, the door slamming so hard behind her that it rattled the frame nearly as much as it did her mother. Linda wrung her hands and tried to slow her breathing in the silence left behind by her daughter.

The nerve of Sarah, invoking the age-old argument, *Dad would let me go.* As if Gary ever approve such a frivolous field trip when they were so short on cash. Linda couldn't help her next thought: It was Gary's fault they were in such a mess, anyway. If only he made a better living, maybe they could afford Sarah's field trip to Paris.

Linda looked up as Jake flew down the stairs into the living room, jumping the broken step at the bottom. His sneakers streaked dirt across the old wooden floors, dislodging from the soles after some soccer game or another. He was always forgetting his cleats, worn as they were to hardly make a difference in his performance.

"Don't worry about her, Mom." He grabbed his backpack from its place on the faded leather couch. "She'll come around."

"Thanks, Jake." She sometimes wondered if their older son understood more than they realized, despite her efforts to keep their financial troubles from the kids. They had enough on their plates without worrying about her and Gary's mistakes.

Jake followed his sister outside to the old beater they drove to school, leaving Linda alone in the house with her thoughts. She wiped a trickle of sweat from her forehead and glanced longingly at the ancient air conditioner in the window. The thing was so old that the minimal relief was hardly worth the strain on their electric bill in this lingering summer heat wave.

Linda crossed the kitchen to the box of vegetables on the counter, the red-rimmed logo unchanged since her childhood. What was inside this week? Whatever her uncle included, she'd make it work. She always did, and for half the price she'd pay for produce at Scott's Grocery in town.

She removed a few carrots from the pile and set them beside the sink while she gathered her peeler and a small ceramic bowl. The bright orange scraps fell to the bottom, soon to be joined by whatever other remnants she could salvage for this week's vegetable stock.

The peeled carrots rolled along the cutting board as she slid her favorite knife smoothly from its block. She fingered the handle, letting it invoke old memories of Gary surprising her with the expensive tool so long ago, just when she'd accepted she could never afford it. It felt like a different lifetime, overcome as she was by love for him back then.

The knife sliced effortlessly through the carrots, transforming them into a pile of perfectly uniform medallions. Linda collected them into a yellowing container and stored them in the refrigerator, wrinkling her nose at the rotting waste of weeks-old dinner leftovers as she closed the door.

Her phone buzzed on the counter.

"Hello?"

"Linda Jones?"

"Yes. Who is this?"

"This is Dave from Cove Harbor bank. I'm making a

7

courtesy call to let you know your checking account is overdrawn. You are showing a negative balance, and there will be a $25 fee for the overdraft."

"Seriously?" Linda replied, "When someone runs out of money, you charge them more? How is that fair?"

"I'm sorry, ma'am. That is the bank's policy."

"Right," she conceded. An argument wouldn't get her anywhere with this representative. "Which account is it?"

"The one ending in 8903."

That didn't make any sense. 8903 was their emergency fund. They never took money from that account, especially not without consulting one another. Could it be a fraudulent charge? She couldn't think of any good reason for Gary to withdraw that money.

"Ma'am?"

"Sorry. Yes, okay. I'll take care of it."

Linda hung up without waiting for Dave's response. She dropped her phone back on the counter and climbed the stairs to Gary's crooked desk, tucked neatly into the alcove of the second-floor hallway. Gary hated when she went through his things, but she needed to find their latest bank statement.

She ruffled through the loose papers and unopened envelopes piled disorderly on the worn surface, each stack threatening to topple with her movements. Finally, she found a sealed envelope from the bank, tearing it open and slowly unfolding the paper. She scanned the list of withdrawals, shock and dread washing over her as her eyes moved down the page.

Why had Gary taken out so much money?

Most of the transactions were ATM withdrawals dating back to mid-August. Two were on the debit card, one for a restaurant two towns over, and one for a jewelry store called Elements. She remembered the shop's name, glancing at her freshwater pearl bracelet with its light-catching red stone. The name had been imprinted on the box when Gary gave it to her for her birthday last fall.

But... wait a minute, Linda thought, staring at the date of the transaction. That didn't make any sense. He'd purchased her bracelet nearly a year ago, and this purchase was made on August 16th, just weeks earlier. Could it be an early birthday gift? She supposed that was possible, though frivolous given the state of their finances.

She returned her attention to the restaurant charge. She recognized the Italian restaurant on the bank statement, but she and Gary had never eaten there, and certainly not just a few weeks ago. An unpleasant sensation rising in her stomach, Linda moved to the desk drawers. She pulled them open and rummaged within, unsure what she hoped to find.

She yanked the handle of the bottom drawer, the final one undisturbed, but it stuck hard. She pulled again but still met resistance, rattling the handle in an unsuccessful attempt to jimmy it closed. Peering closer, she realized the problem, then sat back on her heels in surprise.

She'd never known her husband to lock a drawer before.

Linda stood, pushing sweaty bangs off her forehead, and

walked briskly to Gary's nightstand in their bedroom. She opened the skinny top drawer to reveal a blank notepad and a stray lighter — nothing out of the ordinary. A pack of gum had melted into the wood towards the back, discoloring it. She frowned in irritation, knowing it would be her who scrubbed it out.

Next, she tried the pockets of his flannels in the closet and his pants in the drawer. She slid her hand under his side of the mattress, realizing as she did so that she would already know if there was a key hidden in any of these places. After all, she did the laundry and made the beds. She returned to his desk, thinking hard.

Linda and Gary had been together since they were 19 and known one another even longer. Where would he stash a key? He wasn't the type to hide it in plain sight, but he also liked items convenient for their purpose. She ran her fingers slowly and carefully along the underside of the desktop.

There! A lump!

She yanked on it hard, and it tore from the wood. The key had been affixed to the bottom of the desk with a simple piece of scotch tape, held tight just inches from the drawer it secured. Linda peeled off the clear plastic and slid the key into the lock.

It clicked as it turned, and she held her breath.

Unlike the overflowing mess of the desk's other compartments, this one was nearly barren. She reached for a dark blue notebook resting atop a neat pile of papers, flipping it open with a gasp of surprise. It was a simple ledger of names, dates, and amounts.

She could hardly believe her eyes.

Gary had been borrowing money from their friends and family members for years and, as far as she could tell, hadn't paid any of them back. She rubbed her forehead, feeling the beginnings of a migraine there. This was bad. This was really bad.

With an unshakable sense of foreboding, Linda laid the notebook to one side and rifled through the papers. They were an odd collection of receipts for various updates and services for the fishing boat. A group of notes and printed emails lay underneath, along with an old photograph.

A messy note was scribbled over the familiar faces of herself, Gary, Jim Morris, and Jim's younger sister, Sam, arms around one another, the high school homecoming bonfire roaring behind them.

C'mon, man. We go way back.

Perplexed, she returned the photograph to its place, trying to remember the last time they'd seen the two oldest Morris siblings. It was long enough that she couldn't recall even the smallest details. She recognized Jim's handwriting, probably always would, considering how often she'd seen it over their adolescence.

She looked into Jim's frozen eyes, distracted momentarily by everything that could have been. Not for the first time, but certainly with the most fervor, she wondered if she'd made the right choice in Gary. It had seemed like it then, trading in Jim's impulsive ways for Gary's promised stability.

A home. A family. A predictable life with an up-and-coming fisherman, set to inherit a stable business and a strong future from his family. Her sense of foreboding increased, as if her instincts knew before she did that it was all about to come crashing down.

Linda sighed, lifting the final papers from the drawer. Something colorful fluttered to the floor as she did so, bright even in this shadowed alcove. She eyed the little pink card for a moment before picking it up.

Thank you for a perfect evening.

Can't wait to do it again soon. xx. Julia.

"Who the fuck is Julia?" Linda said aloud, angry tears starting now in her eyes. They pooled, nearly spilling over her cheeks as she flung the card to the floor and shot to her feet. It all made sense now. The missing money. The jewelry. The restaurant. Tears began in her eyes and she wiped them away, violently tearing at her skin. She wouldn't cry for him, not now, not -

"Mom?"

"Jake!" Linda reeled as her son emerged from his bedroom down the hall. "What are you doing here?!"

"I forgot my cleats. I have soccer today..." Jake spoke

slowly, his sentence trailing into an uncomfortable silence.

"Oh, right." She forced a smile. "Did you find them?"

"Mom, what are you doing in Dad's desk?" He hadn't bothered answering her question, but she didn't blame him, the cleats swaying lightly between them as he tightly clutched their laces.

"Just looking for something," Linda replied, hoping Jake wouldn't notice her red eyes or pounding heart. Beads of sweat dotted on her forehead.

It was so damn *hot* in this house.

Linda turned back to Gary's desk, grasping at anything she could hold, anything to normalize the moment. She lifted a random collection of discarded mail, waving it in Jake's direction.

"Ah, here it is. Nothing important."

"Who's Julia?" Her son's voice shook as he asked the question, not with real curiosity, but with an obligation that told Linda he already knew the answer.

Her heart sank as she imagined Jake discovering the other woman on his own, hiding it from her, grappling with his father's deception as he protected their family. Linda's fingers tightened on the mail, crumpling the edges as she struggled to tear her eyes from the envelopes, to meet her son's gaze.

What could she say to him? Could she bring herself to confirm his fears, to admit to her son that his dad was a liar? A liar, a swindler, *and* a cheat. It was almost too much to voice into the world.

"Mom?"

Her churning anger turned to cold fury as she realized the full impact of Gary's betrayal, not only of her but of their children, and everything they built together. She could kill him for this. She waited a moment, letting the rage stamp out any remnants of her earlier hurt, then smiled, meeting Jake's eyes.

"Don't worry, Jake. It's going to be okay."

JIM MORRIS

September 16
12:54 PM

The machine's steady beeping filled his ears, reminding Jim his mother was still alive. Physically, at least. The cancer was spreading, and although she hadn't succumbed to the dementia that claimed so many her age, his mother's misery had sapped her spirits so entirely she was hardly recognizable.

"How was your morning, Mom?" he asked. As if he didn't already know.

"Terrible," she replied, hoarse with disgust. "They've closed the chapel and the eggs are like rubber. If your poor father could see me like this... He's rolling in his grave, I'm sure."

"I know, Mom. I'm sorry," Jim replied, "I'm doing my best to get you somewhere else. We're still waiting for the financial aid to come through. Everywhere is so expensive, and we - "

"You know what else is expensive?" His mother's croaky voice cut through his excuses as easily as they had when he was still in middle school. "Raising four kids! But I did that, so wouldn't you think you could figure it out like your father and I did for all those years?"

He couldn't bring himself to argue with her. She didn't understand why she was stuck in this falling-down care home that couldn't even keep the lights on in the chapel. If he continued these visits, the guilt was bound to swallow him whole, but what else could he do? She was his mother, and none of this was her fault.

"I'm sorry," Jim said again.

His life was a series of bad decisions, and he had only himself to blame for their family's predicament. He was the oldest, and the only one of his siblings without his own family to provide for. The responsibility of their ailing mother was undoubtedly his, and boy did he fail to live up to it. Once a fuck up, always a fuck up. He knew that's what they all thought of him.

Anger bubbled beneath the surface, but he swallowed it whole, breathing deeply and counting slow numbers like he practiced in counseling. Inhale for three, exhale for six. Repeat. The smell of antiseptic and old age made him want to gag.

"Can I get you anything, Mom?"

No response.

He stood anyway and retrieved a blanket from the old armchair by the window, his thumb pushing clear through the thin fabric to the other side. He lay it over her legs, promising himself he'd purchase another as soon as he could.

"Is that better?"

"It's fine," she replied, averting her eyes.

Jim sensed her pain, with her stiff legs and the cancer eating her from the inside almost as aggressively as the lonely abandonment of this place she now called home. His father stared at him from his frame on the bedside table, the familiar expression lodging something in Jim's throat. His old man would be ashamed of him for letting their mother live this way.

"Hi, guys!" His sister's cheery voice broke the emptiness, lighting up the room and his mother's face with her sunny demeanor. "Nice day, isn't it?"

At least Sam could still cheer up their mother.

"Samantha!" Jim watched his mom beckon Sam forward, cracking her first smile of the day for her only daughter. "You're here!"

Arms full of paper bags from Scott's grocery, Sam bent to kiss their mother on the cheek, her golden hair falling in Irish curls over her face. She withdrew a trim bouquet of flowers for their mother's empty vase, something Jim never would have remembered.

"Have we eaten lunch?" she asked, piling sandwiches onto the rolling tray table.

"Oh, now, Samantha," their mother replied, "You know I'm not supposed to eat those."

"Live a little, Mom!"

She passed around napkins, avoiding Jim's eyes. They both knew their mother's condition had deteriorated so rapidly that this sandwich was the least of her worries.

Samantha's arrival brought easier conversation, stories of her ten-year-old son, and tales of her escapades managing Reels, a restaurant downtown. She was so much better than him at the forced bedside conversation that accompanied this stage of his once stoic mother's life.

An hour later, Jim sat in the care home parking lot scrolling through search results.

High quality elder care for cancer patients.

Elder care facilities near me.

Nursing homes for aging Catholic women.

It was an exercise in futility, as he already knew none were in their price range. He'd applied for government aid, but it wasn't likely to be approved until too late.

He closed his search and opened his bank app, one glance confirming what he already knew. Jim had hardly enough for his own mortgage payment, let alone to move his mother somewhere nicer. But he had to do *something*. He couldn't live with himself if this were how she spent her final months on Earth.

Jim jumped as someone tapped the passenger side window.

"Let me in." It was Sam.

He unlocked the door, allowing his sister to slide into the passenger seat. Her eyes lingered on his account page and he quickly darkened the screen.

"Hey," he said, shoving his phone into the car's cup holder.

"We need to do something about this." Sam gestured to the worn brick exterior of the building.

"I know," Jim replied, rubbing his eyes. "I just don't think we have many options."

Sam stared at him silently. Expectantly.

"What about Nick and Carl?" Jim asked. He hadn't worked up the nerve to talk to either of them in weeks. He wouldn't have spoken to Sam, either, if she hadn't shown up here today.

"Nick is strapped with the boys' college tuition – Did you hear that Will is going to school in North Carolina next year? - and you know Carl is hardly keeping a roof over their heads with the auction house struggling." Sam looked down at her lap. "I'm giving everything I can, but it's not enough."

She didn't have to say it, Jim thought bitterly. He was the one not pulling his weight, like always.

"I'm sorry, Sam, I just - "

"Where's the money, Jim?"

"What money?" A cold drop of sweat materialized on his neck.

"The money you got from selling the house in the village. That money was for Mom, and you know it. Dad only gave you control over the place so we could use the sale money in this exact situation. We've been trying to give you the benefit of the doubt, Jim, but *what happened to the money?*"

"Don't worry about it, Sam. Just leave it alone."

"This has gone on long enough! Normally, I wouldn't care about your stupid decisions, but this was family money, not yours! And if you're holding out on us..."

"I'm not!" Jim insisted, anger swelling into that familiar, unwelcome pressure preceding an explosion. He clenched his fists, trying to count his breathing.

Inhale, 1, 2, 3...

But it was pointless. He'd never been able to keep the violence inside. Who was he kidding, thinking he could control it? That some lady with a clipboard could fix it?

"Jim! Don't lie to me!"

"I'm not lying!" Jim roared, losing control of his voice, "I don't have it!"

"Then, where is it!?" Sam's own temper stilled Jim somehow, and he closed his eyes, swallowing what he could of the rage, pushing it deep into his belly. "Jim?!"

"It's gone, okay? I lent it to that snake, Gary, and he hasn't given it back!" He slammed his fist on the dashboard, making her jump. "It's gone!"

"Calm down!" She put two fingers to her temple. "Gary Jones? From high school? The one who married Linda?"

"Yes, Gary Jones! What other Gary do we know?" Jim grew even hotter under the collar at the reminder of Gary's marriage to Linda. "Goddamnit!"

"Tell me what happened, Jim." Sam's anger was quieter than his own, but he could feel it in the car, thick and palpable enough to cut with a knife. "Tell me right now, so help me..."

"I gave it to him for his boat, and he promised to have it back in a year with interest. I thought it'd be a good way to make some money off it, what with the interest he promised and all. But it's been three years and nothing, nada, zilch."

Sam didn't reply. He knew she wouldn't understand. His level-headed sister would never do something so unbelievably stupid. Stupid *and* reckless. Jim would, though. Stupid and reckless might as well be his middle name.

"I didn't know we would need it like this! I swear, Sam, I didn't. And I never imagined he wouldn't pay me back. He seemed so sincere, and I thought we could put old differences aside for a mutually beneficial deal."

"Have you asked him for it?" Sam asked, cutting across his explanations.

"Asked him?! Of course I have! I've been hounding him for the better part of a year. But he's dodging me, and when I manage to get a hold of him, he says he doesn't have it yet."

Sam's eyes darted around the car before she squeezed them shut, returning her fingers to her temple. She inhaled deeply through her nose.

"Well, you need to get it back, Jim," Sam finally said. "Because I'm not exactly made of money, you know, and the account I've been using to pay for this place is just about dried up. It's the end of the line."

Jim stared at her, lost for words. He wanted to promise he would get it back. That everything would be okay. But he couldn't. He had no idea how to do that. He was helpless. Sam met his eyes, and he knew she couldn't think less of him.

She opened the door and left without another word, slamming it hard behind her.

Jim watched her old sedan pull out of the parking lot before turning the key in the ignition, his temper flaring again. He slammed on the gas and peeled out of the parking lot, hot wrath clouding his thoughts as he sped towards the local pub.

This wasn't his fault. Not really.

It was Gary Jones' fault, and he would make him pay.

WALTER KENT

September 16
3:32 AM

Walter's email sounded with that shrill, incessant chime that would one day send him over the edge. He smashed the mute button on his company computer and leaned back in his chair, twisting his back into a stretch that cracked something it wouldn't have five years ago.

Boredom dragged him downward, deeper into the lumbar support pillow of his office chair. He'd been answering emails all day, an unfortunate side effect of the pharmaceutical company he'd inherited from his father, and there seemed no end in sight. No wonder the old man retired early.

He checked his phone, but still nothing from Julia. It wasn't like his wife to be so out of touch. Even when she wasted away September weeks at the summer house, she still typically checked in, usually bothered to text. Sometimes even to the point of annoyance during his solo time in the city.

Julia had taken a new liking to Cove Harbor this summer. Walter knew it was more carnal than she'd let on, but who was he to complain? After all, he never exactly shied away from a conquest himself, so what did he care if his wife was sleeping with some fisherman while he was away? It didn't matter.

Walter returned to his inbox, skimming for anything requiring immediate attention. Maybe he'd leave early and visit one of the nicer lounges uptown. If Julia was out getting hers, why shouldn't he do the same? Just as he was about to close his computer, his phone vibrated, buzzing gently against the hard surface of his desk.

"Joe. What's up?"

"We have a situation, sir."

Joe always maintained a level of calm that left Walter eternally unsure of the magnitude of any 'situation.' Still, hiring the ex-Navy Seal had been one of the best decisions of his young career. In a business like his, Walter liked the peace of mind of the security detail, not to mention the convenience of a driver in the crowded city.

"What kind of situation?"

"I think it's best if you see for yourself. Come on down to the security room on the IT floor."

"Be there in five."

Walter hung up, slamming his computer shut as he stood.

He passed his secretary on the way out, returning her smile with a wave and one of his own. He couldn't resist a small wink that made her blush as he rounded the corner. She was cute, and learning his routines surprisingly quickly for a new hire.

Walter hurried to the elevator. What would cause Joe to summon him like this? It must be something serious. It had been only a few weeks since he'd last spoken with any of the doctors on the unofficial payroll, and all had seemed in order. He shook his head, chiding himself for always jumping to the worst conclusions.

Walter was through the elevator doors before they'd finished opening, hurrying to join Joe on the other side. Their shoes clicked loudly against the gray stone floor as he fell into step beside the larger man.

"What's going on, Joe?"

"You need to see for yourself," Joe repeated.

They entered a circular room dotted with wide monitors and blinking equipment. Walter followed Joe to the back of the space, where a bespectacled man in a purple tie sat behind a large, thin desktop.

"Take a look at this," Joe said, gesturing to the screen. "There."

Walter peered over Purple Tie's shoulder. It was footage from the front cameras, recorded late enough at night to appear dull and gray. He watched Julia enter the building, one hand tightly clutching her handbag. A few clicks later, another frame followed her into the elevator, and then across his office.

She perched on the edge of his chair, jamming something into the USB slot of his computer. Her fingers moved lightly over the trackpad, maneuvering around his screen, while her foot tapped incessantly beneath the desk. She remained there for a few minutes before retrieving her USB drive and leaving the room.

Walter resisted the urge to panic as the footage rolled. It didn't take an IT professional to see that his wife secretly downloaded something from his computer in the dead of night. But how could this be? Julia wasn't even in the city.

"Wait... When is this from?" Walter coughed, hoping to mask the fear and confusion in his voice. "Julia is at the beach house this week."

"That's part of the concern, sir," Joe replied. "This footage is from last night."

Tension cramped Walter's shoulders as he looked back at the screen. What did she take from his computer? Could it be what he thought it was? Panic turned his stomach.

"Can we find out what she downloaded?!" The words rushed out faster than he intended and he steadied himself before continuing. He didn't want Purple Tie to know how worried he was about his wife's bizarre behavior. "I mean, is there a digital record?"

"Already done, Mr. Kent," Purple Tie replied, "I sent everything to Mr. Smith."

Joe nodded. "I have it, sir. I suggest we go somewhere more private to discuss the matter further."

Walter nodded and left the room without another word, leading Joe back to his office upstairs. He sat on the brown patent couch and looked expectantly at Joe.

"So?"

Joe handed him a tablet.

"This is what she was looking at."

Walter's heart sank as he scrolled through the documents on the screen. How could he have been so stupid? He never should have trusted her.

"We believe she downloaded the files."

As if Walter hadn't just watched her do it with his own eyes.

"But why?!" Walter exclaimed, rising to his feet. "Why would she do this?"

"Do you remember the problem I came to you about over the summer? About what Mrs. Kent was doing at the beach house?"

"The fisherman?"

Impatience nagged at Walter. What did Julia's fisherman have to do with anything? Surely, he couldn't be behind any of this. He was just a fisherman, a local nobody from their summer town.

"Yes, sir. I took the liberty of reviewing Mrs. Kent's recent phone activity, and I believe she is planning to run away with him."

"And what? Blackmail me?" Walter laughed at the absurdity of the idea. "No way! I mean, sure, Julia seems to like the guy, but that's ridiculous." There's no way Julia would choose that old fisherman over him - not when the guy was dead broke. His wife liked a certain lifestyle, that's for sure, and it hadn't taken long for Walter to learn the sorry state of her beau's finances.

Then, a darker thought crossed his mind. Maybe Julia thought she could force enough money out of him to keep her and her townie happy for years to come. Well, if that's what she thought, she couldn't be more wrong. He was no pushover. His father, for all his faults, had taught him well.

"I need a drink," Walter said as Joe opened his mouth to speak again. "Let's get out of here."

He followed Joe down to the Bentley and collapsed into the backseat, his mind on overdrive. Walter couldn't believe it. Julia would never betray him like this. She *wouldn't*. But... she'd definitely downloaded the list of doctors and the payment records from the last five years. He never would have believed it if he didn't see the film for himself, but he had seen it. There could be no doubt.

Walter dialed her number repeatedly as they drove, asking himself question after question he couldn't answer. Would the documents be enough to implicate him if he were investigated? How serious of a crime was it to pay doctors in exchange for prescribing Kent Pain Management medications? It wasn't his fault if patients became addicted to their pills. At least, that's what his father used to say.

They pulled up to Walter's favorite lounge, an old-fashioned place uptown that looked more like a twentieth-century speakeasy than anything else. He'd met Julia here in the beginning, sought her out from across the room, though he thought he might've noticed her from across the city, the way she stood out in a crowd.

Walter glanced at her contact photo, jamming the call button again. He knew by now that she wouldn't pick up, but had to try one last time before stepping out onto the sidewalk. Joe closed the door behind him and Walter headed inside, ready for a stiff drink to calm his nerves.

He glanced back as he approached the glass doors. His eyes lingered on the shiny gold decal stuck to the back of the car. It was a magnetic version of the company logo, stuck there on the bumper for all to see. Walter remembered when Julia put it there, laughing at her joke about free marketing.

She would never do this to him, he thought. Never.

Walter looked at Joe, still waiting by the car.

"Joe?"

"Yes, sir?"

"Take care of the problem. *She* was never the problem. Understand?"

"Yes, sir. Enjoy your drink."

And with that, Walter stepped through the glass doors of the lounge, letting them close silently behind him. He wouldn't see Joe for a few days, but that was to be expected. By the time they met again, the issue would be resolved, and Julia would be home again.

JULIA KENT

September 16
9:35 PM

Julia was giddy as she beamed across the table, drunk on champagne, love, and the promise of so many wonderful things to come. A red flower decorated her dark curls, perfectly complimented by scarlet lipstick and the stone in her freshwater pearl bracelet. A brown clutch sat on the table and she was hyper-aware of the USB drive within it, like a glowing talisman of freedom and opportunity tucked safely inside the quilted leather.

Julia raised her glass to Gary, his blue eyes shining across the table.

"What are we toasting, love?" Gary asked, a tipsy smile crossing his face.

"Our future, Gary!" Julia replied, unable to stop herself from laughing out loud. "I've finally done it! Our life together is underway!"

Gary smiled wide and clinked his glass against hers, but she couldn't help but notice the hesitant question in his eyes. No matter. He would understand soon enough. They drained their glasses, Julia resting the empty flute beside her steak knife, forgotten when it should have been collected with their dinner plates. She waved at their server, a young blonde man leaning against the bar, and beckoned him over.

"Could we have another bottle, please?"

Gary raised his eyebrows but did not protest.

"Of course!" The server smiled, likely anticipating his tip growing ever larger with each request. It reminded Julia of her days working at the lounge before she married Walter, though she'd been much better at the job than this young man.

Never again, she thought, patting her clutch.

Julia smiled as their bottle arrived and their glasses filled, the champagne pairing so well with the chocolate mousse in front of her. Maybe she should feel bad for spending Walter's money this way. Or maybe she shouldn't, considering his role in the misfortune of so many.

She still burned inside at the memory of his confession, shared too easily, with a little bit of pride and not nearly enough shame. Julia's brother was on her mind then and now, the stillness of his coffin, of their home, of everything after he finally lost his hopeless battle with heroin. She didn't think her mother ever really recovered, still deafened and paralyzed by the silence.

Years of pain. Years of struggle, and endless regret. Of programs and rehab centers, therapists and every experimental treatment their family could afford. It was all for nothing in the end. And their long nightmare had begun with a simple car accident.

A car accident, and an opioid prescription.

She'd fallen out of love with Walter as he explained the source of his family fortune in that secluded rooftop garden last winter. Their kickbacks to the doctors, his father's insistence that other people's addictions weren't their problem. It made sense now, why he'd been so tightlipped about his business, why he'd never answered her questions properly. She'd thought it was because he felt guilty about selling prescription medication. She couldn't have been more wrong.

If Walter thought the revelation would strengthen their young marriage, he was sorely mistaken. Although to be fair, he never knew of her brother. She didn't like to speak of him, nor those evil little pills, and Julia kept her secrets close throughout the whirlwind affair that carried them to the altar.

"Julia?" Gary's voice interrupted her thoughts. Why was she dwelling on the past? None of that mattered now. Gary would never do such a thing, never hurt so many people. He could never be so cruel, this kind man in front of her.

"Sorry," Julia replied, offering him a bite of her chocolate. "My mind is all over the place tonight!"

Gary chuckled and accepted the dessert from her fork.

"Anything important?" he asked, wiping his mouth with his napkin.

"Actually, yes!" Julia was happier than she'd been in years as she prepared her announcement. She couldn't wait to see her own joy reflected in Gary's earnest face.

"Hmmm?" Gary prompted, intertwining his fingers with hers across the table.

"I've done it, Gary! I've found a way for us to be together forever!"

Gary tilted his head questioningly. He didn't speak.

"Like, forever, forever! And the best part is, we'll be set for life! You'll never work another day. And we won't have to worry about Walter or Linda ever again! We can leave Cove Harbor! Together!"

"Woah... Hang on, Julia." Gary withdrew his hand. "What do you mean?"

"I've taken what I need to ensure Walter keeps the money coming for a long time. I'll tell him this weekend that I'm leaving. You do the same with Linda, and by Monday morning, we will be free!"

"Wait a minute, Julia – " Gary wasn't smiling anymore. "I never asked you to do that."

"But you said," Julia began, her own smile faltering. "You've been saying all summer... If it weren't for Linda and Walter, we could be together..."

"I can't just leave! What about my kids? And Linda... Well, I could never do that to her. Not for real, Julia. I thought you understood... I thought you knew..." Gary trailed off, but

Julia wasn't listening anymore.

Humiliation flooded her, burning hot from head to toe. The champagne that amplified her elation just a few minutes ago now churned in her stomach. She was going to be sick. She jumped to her feet, kicking back her chair, and fled, her hand clamped tightly over her mouth.

She flung open the bathroom door and sunk to her knees, vomiting violently into the toilet. She remained on the floor afterward, her head propped in her hands, wishing she could vanish into the spinning room. After a few minutes, Julia pulled herself to her feet. She flushed away the sick and stared at herself in the mirror.

"This doesn't need to be the end," she told her reflection. "Clean up, get yourself together, and get back out there!" There's no way Gary would choose his sad little washed-up wife over her. Not if she could help it.

Julia tousled her hair, letting it fall loose around her shoulders. She splashed cold water on her cheeks, rinsed her mouth, and wiped away the dark makeup running under her eyes. She slid the cover from the tube of lipstick in her pocket, dashing a few swipes across her lips, and she was ready, standing tall as she left the restroom.

Julia's heart sank, however, as she approached their table. Her clutch remained, accompanied only by her half-eaten chocolate mousse and leftover champagne.

Gary was gone.

Unsure what else to do, Julia took her seat. She poured what was left of the bottle into her glass and drank, praying to a god she didn't believe in that the alcohol would end the pain in her chest. It sloshed over the rim as she returned it to the table, staining the white linen beside her steak knife.

She felt like the stupid little girl Gary probably thought she was - Just some bored trophy wife, naive enough to believe the lies of an older married man. She chased another pang in her chest with a large gulp of champagne.

Julia couldn't be sure how long she sat at the table ordering drinks. The longer she remained in the restaurant, staring at Gary's empty chair, the angrier she became. She had risked everything for him. Put herself in jeopardy for him, over and over again. If she'd been caught last night... Well, she shuddered just thinking about it.

And Gary didn't care! He'd thrown her away faster than piece of old fishing line. He'd chosen his pathetic wife over her in less than a heartbeat.

Before she knew what she was doing, she dropped four crisp hundred-dollar bills on the table and rose, phone in hand. She swiped away 36 missed calls from Walter without a second thought and opened her car service app.

Julia knew where Gary was, could picture the marina in Cove Harbor where he always sought to untangle his thoughts. She found it on the map, typed in the address, and slugged back the end of her glass.

She'd show *him*, she thought drunkenly, hostility concentrating inside her like some guiding beacon. She'd show Gary Jones what happened to anyone who had the nerve to cross her.

GARY JONES

September 16
11:28 PM

Gary paced another long, slow path across the grassy field beside the marina, staring out over the water. He needed to clear his head, and this unusual marina was his favorite place to do just that. A paved road encircled a wide grass field just off the village Main Street. Boats docked along the north side, a level below the park itself, accessible by a series of ladders from the grass down to the wooden docks.

Gary stood on the edge and watched the boats anchored in the distance, little more than shadows and blinking lights in the night. Directly in front of him floated a row of fancy sailboats. They were the kind a wealthier man than himself lounged on, not designed for making a living, or hauling in a commercial catch.

They were beautiful, though. There was no denying it.

A dark-colored Bentley entered the nearby parking lot, its

engine disturbing the quiet of the night. Gary watched in annoyance as it made a u-turn, an obnoxious gold logo turning towards him. It looked strangely familiar, but he couldn't remember where he'd seen it before. He shouldn't have drank so much champagne.

"Gary!"

He groaned as Julia's angry voice cut through the peace. He pulled his eyes from the Bentley and turned to face her.

Even as he dreaded what was to come, Gary couldn't help but admire her figure as she stalked towards him in her tall heels. He remembered how the skinny things caught his attention that first night in May, so different from the local forty-somethings he was accustomed to seeing at Kelly's Pub.

"Don't shout, Julia, please..."

"Don't you dare tell me what to do, Gary Jones!"

Damn, she was drunk, Gary realized, extending an arm to steady her. She smacked his hand away angrily. She was *really* drunk.

"DON'T touch me, you asshole!"

"Jeez, sorry, I was just trying to —"

"I don't care what you were trying to do, Gary! You're a nasty liar, and I'm finished with you! I can't believe I ever trusted you! Ever *wanted* you!"

Her words cut through Gary like ice, but he knew he deserved them. Then again, what was he supposed to do? He couldn't leave Linda and the kids; that was never on the table. He thought Julia realized that but, he'd clearly been mistaken.

"Julia, please, try to be reasonable. I have children to think about. I - " He stopped himself, realizing now was not the time to proclaim his love for his wife. "I can't..."

Julia thrust her hand violently inside her bag, and for a moment, Gary saw the flash of something sinister in her eyes. She withdrew a small flash drive and held it up, waving it in front of him.

"You see this!? You have NO IDEA what I've sacrificed for you! None at all! And you just stand there, like the loser you are, in this stupid marina!"

Gary really had no idea what she was going on about now.

As she waved the little memory stick around, her bracelet flew off, landing on the ledge above the boats. She kicked it angrily, and the gift he'd paid for from his emergency savings clattered to the dock below.

"Julia, please - "

She opened her mouth again, readying for her next verbal assault, but then -

"Dad?" A quieter voice interrupted. It wasn't nearly as angry, but Gary thought it more terrifying than anything Julia could possibly say to him.

"Jake? What are you doing here?"

His son walked towards him, hands in his pockets and eyes fixed on Julia.

"So that's her?" He looked disgusted. "Real classy, Dad."

"Jake, please..." Gary turned away from Julia, scared silent by the sight of his boy. He didn't even notice her vanish into the darkness.

"Mom's mad as hell at you, Dad, and I don't really want much to do with you right now, myself. How could you do this?!"

"Jake - " His voice broke, "I'm sorry, I - "

"Jake!" Linda's voice interrupted him, "We're leaving! Now! Get in the car!"

Gary looked around in alarm, realizing that the only thing that could make this situation worse was his wife and his mistress coming face to face. But to his surprise, he didn't see Julia anywhere. He did, however, see the same Bentley he noticed earlier, a burly-looking man in sunglasses watching him intently from the driver's seat.

Linda walked rapidly towards him, her old coat billowing around her favorite sneakers. His heart stopped at the sight of her. He was really in for it now.

"Jake! I said, GO!" His son jumped and turned his back on Gary, following his mother's instructions, disappearing into the night.

"Linda, how did you know I was here - "

"*That's* what you're worried about!?" Linda's eyes flashed. "I could kill you, Gary Jones!"

He bit his tongue, certain anything he said would only make it worse.

Linda turned to make sure Jake was safely in the car before hissing, "Are you happy now? Happy that your son discovered your ugly affair and your evil lies? Happy that he knows what a sneak you are? And don't even get me started on that ledger in your desk. Shameful!"

She reached into the long inside pocket of her jacket and withdrew her kitchen knife. moonlight dancing down the blade. He knew it instantly after months saving to buy it for her. Gary's heart broke a little as he remembered her happy surprise the morning she opened it.

"Linda, what - "

She grasped the knife wordlessly and threw back her arm, hurling it towards the boats as hard as she could. It didn't make it all the way to the water but landed heavily on the wooden slats below.

"Don't come home, Gary! I mean it! I don't want to see your lousy face again."

She spun on her heel and stalked off, leaving him standing alone. He watched her go, shaking his head. Sure, Linda was angry, but she'd get over it. This couldn't be the end. Not for them. Not after so many years.

Gary walked to the edge of the park and climbed slowly down the ladder to the docks. He almost laughed at the sight of the knife and bracelet next to one another on the weathered planks. He'd really made a mess of things, hadn't he?

He approached the knife, intending to pick it up and return it to Linda when she was ready to hear his apology. Before he reached it, however, another figure jumped lightly from a shadowy ladder down the pier.

"Hello?" He called down the dock. "Who's that?!"

"Gary Jones?" It was a woman's voice: familiar but not

immediately recognizable.

"Yes?" he answered. "Who's there?"

"I saw your truck parked down the way." She stepped closer, into the moonlight, and he knew who she was. That golden hair.

"Sam Morris?"

"The one and only," she replied, glancing down at the knife lying between them.

Gary remembered Sam from their high school years. Jim's little sister was a year or so younger, though outspoken and fearless enough to hang out with them often. He'd hit on her once, back when Jim and Linda had still been together. She'd rejected him so solidly, even Jim didn't care enough to confront him about it.

She'd grown up well, he thought, her green eyes glowing in the night. Maybe she'd reconsider him now that he was older and wiser. He knew he probably shouldn't get involved with anyone right now, not with Linda so angry, and definitely not with someone in the Morris family. Then again, he wasn't even sure Sam knew he borrowed money from her brother.

"I heard you borrowed some money from my brother," she said, as if reading his mind.

"Yeah, I did," Gary replied, "But we have an arrangement. No biggie." He laughed softly, hoping to coax a smile from her.

"Here's the thing, Gary," Sam wasn't smiling. "I don't think you have an arrangement. I think you took my family's money, and we need it back."

"It's not happening tonight, Sam," Gary replied, suddenly frustrated. It had been a long night, and he wasn't in the mood for it to get even longer. Especially not at the hands of Jim Morris' little sister, rude as she was.

"I wasn't asking. I need that money and I'm not leaving until we work something out!"

Sam was nearly yelling now, spurred on by that famous Morris temper Gary knew too well. How often had he seen Jim punch a guy's lights out over nothing? He'd even been on the receiving end of it once after he got together with Linda. It must run in the family.

"Look, Sam, I don't have it. If I did, I'd repay the loan." Gary was on the verge of losing control himself, fueled by the champagne and the night's already substantial toll. "But the fact is, your idiot brother made a stupid, unofficial deal, and quite frankly, there's nothing either one of you can do about it. I'll see you around."

He shook his head at her ignorance before turning and walking back towards the ladder. The knife wasn't worth it. He'd get Linda a new one or tell her it landed in the water. It wasn't important.

It happened so fast, Gary never saw it coming. Something in Sam snapped when he laughed at her standing there, asking only for what she was owed and what her mother so desperately needed. Something broke deep inside, the dam giving way to every ounce of pain, every regret, every swallowed bite of anger at her brother and her mother's undeserved suffering.

Sam Morris saw red.

She grabbed the knife from the dock and thrust it into Gary's back, over and over again, until he lay still and motionless before her. She stood, looking down at this man who caused her family so much pain, and felt no remorse or regret. He never would've made enough money to pay them back, anyway.

Sam turned away from Gary Jones' body and returned to her car, dropping the knife in the marina as she went. She pulled off her blood-soaked jacket and sweats, driving home only in her bra and underwear. They went into her furnace, burned to ashes as surely as Gary's life had been, and she never dwelled on them again.

A HOLIDAY HOMICIDE

A PERILOUS PEPPERMINT

December 24
11:30 AM

"Peppermint hot chocolate!"

The barista's voice sang cheerily through the bustling café, joining the festive sounds of sleigh bells jingling, ring-ting-tingling, from the speakers above. Wide swaths of holiday garland draped over nearly every surface, and poinsettia plants decorated the tables. Everything basked in the delightfully delicious aromas of pine needles and brewing coffee.

A line of thickly-clad customers led from the register to the glass doors, some sweating now that they'd stepped in from the cold. A light snow fell on last-minute shoppers hurrying down the sidewalk, sidestepping the smoke swirling from the cigarette of a tight-curled blonde woman.

The barista added the peppermint hot chocolate to the

collection of drinks on the mosaic surface. She had scrawled *Mindy* across the side in messy letters, and the name seemed to glow in the twinkle lights strung above. She paused after the cup left her hand, winking at a brunette woman leaning against the counter.

Though at least a decade apart in age, the barista and the brunette sported the same thick rubber bracelets, green with yellow block letters: *The Cove Harbor School for Excellence*. The older woman, Hannah, gave her student a salute as the girl turned back towards the espresso machine, snatching her next ticket from the line above.

"Excuse me!"

Amy, the curator of Cove Harbor's famous Seabreeze Studio Art Gallery, attempted to move past a white-haired man standing between her and the counter. Bright red plaid stretched across his rounded belly, threatening to pop the gold buttons right off his festive shirt. Instead of moving aside, he picked up the hot chocolate and offered it to her, turning away momentarily as he maneuvered his girth around a rack of mugs.

"Oh, thank you!" Amy replied, her eyes lingering momentarily on the thin scar across the back of his hand. "Would you mind passing the cappuccino, too?"

"Of course." The man grabbed the second cup and handed it to her with an oddly unsettling smile. "Enjoy your coffee."

The drinks warmed Amy's hands as she carried them to her high-top table, but she didn't crack a smile. Today was not one for smiling, at least not for her. She placed the cardboard cups on the table and waved to the spindly blonde outside. Her companion took one final drag before dropping her cigarette to the sidewalk and crushing it beneath her chunky heel.

The woman clomped into the coffee shop, towering high upon thick, unforgiving boots. Her nose perked at the smells of the café, and she wrinkled it, glancing down at the barista as she passed. She perched lightly on the stool opposite Amy, who thought she looked as though the smallest winter wind might be enough to blow her tiny frame into oblivion.

The woman reached for the peppermint hot chocolate and drank deeply from it, smacking her lips loudly before speaking.

"Now, Amy, can I ask why you invited me here? I thought I was perfectly clear last night." Bright pink lipstick marred the matte white of her hot chocolate lid. She sniffed, taking another sip. "I have nothing left to say to you."

Amy's eyes narrowed.

"How can you treat me this way, Mindy?" Amy's voice came like the hiss of steam escaping the barista's machine, still toiling away behind the counter. "We're friends! And you think you're so untouchable, but you should know you can't push me around. I know the one person who you'd most hate to learn your nasty secret. And I've already told him."

For one barely perceptible moment, emotion cascaded across Mindy's pointy features. Confusion, then concern.

Then guilt, and fear. They were all soon replaced, however, by a blank expression, devoid of any reason or intention.

"Mindy?"

But Mindy did not reply. She slumped forward, then toppled to the ground, her hot chocolate crashing down beside her. Brown liquid seeped from the open cup, staining Mindy's white fur and seeping across the oak floor.

"Mindy!" Amy was shouting now, and the large white-haired man rushed over from the counter, wiping his hands on his dark denim pants.

"I'm a doctor!" he cried, kneeling beside Mindy Pringle. He lifted two fingers to her neck. "This woman is dead!"

The barista screamed as Amy fell to her knees beside Mindy. Shouts mingled with musical sleigh bells and running feet as all abandoned their beverages for a closer look, a better view of the woman who'd collapsed in Cove Harbor's most quaint café.

DR. MARV LUGE

December 23
9:00 AM

Dr. Luge's thumb lingered over a modern painting on his screen, geometric shapes crossing each other over a stark white background. His eyes followed the harsh black outline, enjoying the way it allowed the vibrant colors to leap from the canvas. He wanted to learn more about this painting, to ask if it were available for purchase into his private collection. He knew exactly where it would hang.

"Mr. Pringle is ready now."

Nurse Lori's voice brought the doctor back to his surroundings. He'd have plenty of time to browse art when he finished Mr. Pringle's weekly checkup. After all, he already knew which piece would be his after tonight's Santa's Workshop Holiday Auction, and he wouldn't choose another until the Summer Sun Auction in July.

"Thank you, Nurse Lori. We won't be long."

Dr. Luge entered Mr. Pringle's bedroom. A sliver of light passed through a crack between the drapes into the neat room, kept pleasantly warm by the home's smart system. He'd made sure the nurses knew exactly how to keep the old man most comfortable in his final weeks. It was the least he could do, after all.

Mr. Pringle lay in bed, face upturned and sporting a lopsided smile. He was in good spirits today, likely helped by the melodic music trailing from the luxury speakers in each corner. If everyone had access to the resources of this man, few would die without peace. Much was said for access to care, which was, of course, important, but the doctor knew too well the unquantifiable value of simple comforts at the end.

"Merry Christmas Eve Eve, Mr. Pringle!" Dr. Luge said, though he knew the man had no idea the holiday was upon them. He was too far gone now to recognize such things. Still, the doctor whistled *Jingle Bells* as he worked, unable to shake the tune since his morning walk to the coffee shop.

He loved this time of year, and it resonated with him, all the festivity and holiday dinners. He patted his belly, growing rounder each season, now threatening to burst the gold buttons on his favorite holiday shirts. Maybe he'd retire one day, get back in shape. Or maybe he'd continue enjoying every last pleasure in life until he no longer had a chance to do so.

The nurse entered as Dr. Luge opened his bag to withdraw

his supplies. He rolled up his plaid sleeves, green for Christmas, and rifled through the contents. While he rummaged, Nurse Lori examined the readings on a screen beeping steadily alongside Mr. Pringle's bed. She adjusted the wires trailing to her patient and recorded his vitals on her tablet.

Nurse Lori placed the tablet on the rolling table for him to inspect. He glanced quickly at it but did not pick it up.

"He's been stable this morning, Dr. Luge. Nothing out of the ordinary, and no fits or anything reminiscent of delusions. It's hard to believe he's the same person who was hollering conspiracy theories and attacking the medical staff over the summer. I swear, sometimes I think he will pull through, after all."

He returned her smile. There was no need to burst the poor woman's bubble, not after all the care she took in keeping Mr. Pringle well. Or as well as he could be, under the circumstances.

"I'll be outside if you need me." Nurse Lori gave her patient a hopeful smile as she departed, returning to the small lounge attached to Mr. Pringle's sick room.

His wife had long moved into a different bedroom in their massive home, one with a breathtaking view of the polo fields visible from the estate. Her departure from their master suite allowed its transformation into a makeshift medical facility, with all the technology Dr. Luge could dream of and even an attached suite for care staff. A tall medicine cabinet stretched from the floor to the ceiling beside the man's bookshelf, well-stocked with any medication that might help and quite a few more that probably wouldn't.

The doctor was grateful every day that he'd met Mindy Pringle, and for the doors opened to him by caring for her ailing husband. Undeniably, they came with a regrettable relationship with the woman, an uneasy allowance of her into his life and most private affairs. But it was worth it. Many loved her for her beauty, a young 35 to Mr. Pringle's 79, but her cunning was often overlooked, sailing cleanly under the radar.

She was one smart cookie, that Mindy Pringle.

Mr. Pringle coughed loudly from the bed, wet and sputtering. Dr. Luge bent to him, using a tissue from the box on his bedside table to wipe away a drop of spittle. He dropped it into the trash can with two fingers, as if he could catch what the old man had, though he knew he couldn't.

The clouds shifted outside, casting shadows over the scar on his hand.

"Tsk, tsk," the doctor said. And then to himself: Oh, how the mighty have fallen. He remembered Mr. Pringle in his prime, all dark suits and ruthless business acumen. You couldn't amass such a fortune without both, though neither would help him now.

He shifted the blanket off Mr. Pringles wrist, revealing his IV before retrieving a glass syringe from his bag. Unpleasantness jarred him as he injected his patient, but he thought instead of his art collection, and all negativity was replaced by smug satisfaction.

Dr. Luge enjoyed his medical practice, but he'd might as well despise it compared to his passion for the world of fine art. He'd spent decades establishing his gallery, open to other enthusiasts since his twenties. They paid exorbitant fees just to walk his hallowed halls, the revenue funding all the best parts of life, and then some.

His real pride, however, was not the public labyrinth of artistic expression he so loudly, proudly discussed at dinner parties. No, it was the one beneath, housing a collection like none he'd ever seen anywhere else, existing only in rumors for most of his visitors. *That* gallery was for private viewing only, as just one malicious set of eyes could ruin him forever.

"Dr. Luge?" He jumped at Nurse Lori's voice. "Would you like a cup of coffee before you go?"

Dr. Luge returned his syringe to his bag before replying.

"No, thank you, Nurse Lori." He pulled the zipper around the thick leather seam, securing his supplies inside. "I was just about to head out."

"Next time, then," Nurse Lori replied.

"Will I see you at the Holiday Auction tonight?"

"I wish, Dr. Luge. I'll be here with Mr. Pringle. Please take photos, if you can. I'd like to show him the displays. And with your background, I'm sure you know exactly which pieces he'd be most excited to see."

"I'll do my best," Dr. Luge replied. As if Chris Pringle had any sense left to know his nurse was showing him photos, let alone appreciate any particular pieces of art. But he wouldn't say that out loud, especially not to this nurse who seemed to care for the old man so deeply. He bade her goodbye and left the darkened quarters.

A handsome visitor nodded to Dr. Luge as they passed one another in the carpeted hall. His blue eyes danced with mischief, taking clear pleasure in the doctor's discomfort at seeing him. Dr. Luge swallowed the impropriety of this man's presence in Mr. Pringle's home, especially considering the nature of his relationship with Mindy.

Still, he forced a smile and a curt nod. It wouldn't do to insult him, not with all he knew of the doctor's secrets. They could each ruin the other, if they were so inclined. The idea did little to calm his nerves.

Dr. Luge's phone rang as he descended the stone steps in the foyer.

"Hello?"

"Hi, Dr. Luge. It's Mindy."

"Hello, Mindy. How are you?"

"Doing well, thank you. Have you seen my husband yet? I hoped to catch you before you checked in on him today."

"I am just leaving your home, actually. He's resting now."

"I see." There was a long pause before Mindy continued. "I've just left my attorney's office. Thank you for your help and the documentation you provided. I was able to secure the power of attorney to fully manage Chris' affairs and to make the changes we discussed."

"That's great news, Mindy. It was no trouble at all. He is

not in any state to be making important decisions right now. I find it appalling that they even hassled you over the whole thing."

"Thank you for saying that." Mindy sighed deeply into the phone. "How did he look today?"

"About the same. No significant change."

"As expected. I take it you know what to do next?"

"Of course. I'll return in a few days to provide the dose you requested."

"Perfect. Thank you, doctor."

"No problem, Mindy." He paused for a moment. "And I take it the other aspects of our arrangement have already been put into place?"

"Of course, Doctor." He could almost hear Mindy smiling. "There is nothing left to do but wait."

HANNAH BAILEY

December 23
10:30 AM

Hannah couldn't help but crane her neck, ever awed by the majestic Pringle home pitched against the cold blue December sky. No matter how often she visited, the wonder never fully subsided. Mr. Pringle's home was larger than any other she'd visited, larger even than the school grounds, though it housed only her mentor and his wife.

Hannah pulled her sweatshirt closer as she trotted up the steps, obscuring the yellow lettering across the front – the same as those on her bracelet. Everyone on this property knew what it said anyway, as The Cove Harbor School for Excellence had been Mr. Pringle's pet project since his earliest days of success.

And thank goodness for that, Hannah thought, ringing the bell.

The chimes echoed through the front hall, bouncing off

the shiny stone floor, around the wide curves of the double staircase, and right back to meet her as the heavy doors opened.

"Welcome, welcome, Hannah. Come inside."

Harry beckoned with his neatly manicured hand. She was hit immediately by warmth, born as much from Harry's eyes on hers as from the heat of the Pringle home. The winter chill faded away as she crossed the threshold, Harry's smile dulling even the atmosphere of anxiety that had settled here since Mr. Pringle fell ill.

"Thank you, Harry," she said, patting him on the arm. He'd been Mr. Pringle's assistant as long as she'd been the school's Director of Development, and they were familiar. She wished they were a little more familiar, if she were honest, but the timing never seemed right.

"Anytime," he said, grinning. "It's getting chilly out there."

"Well, that's December, isn't it?"

"True, true. You're here to visit, then?"

"Yep. I wanted to stop in before the holiday." She glanced up the stairs. "How is he today?"

"The same." Harry shrugged. "Pretty much out of it."

She sighed. "Yeah." It wasn't a surprise. Mr. Pringle had been asleep or basically so for the better part of the last six months.

"You can head on up." Then, he lowered his voice and eyes towards her. "Meredith is in the library."

She flushed, giggling at the inside joke, a reference to a character from one of her favorite movies as a child.

Meredith Blake, the famous gold-digger. Mindy Pringle, just the same. In their eyes, anyway.

Hannah left Harry in the foyer, taking the stairs two at a time on her way to Mr. Pringle's quarters. She slowed as she made her way down the hall, suddenly reluctant to see Mr. Pringle lying as he was in that big bed. It was the only one she'd ever known that could make such a broad, powerful man seem frail.

Mr. Pringle had selected her from a pool of candidates when she was hardly out of undergrad, seeing a potential in her that she hadn't quite seen herself. He coached her for the role at his new school, and she thrived there, happily dedicating herself to those who were exactly who she'd been before. An academically-inclined, highly motivated local kid from Cove Harbor, but one without a fancy family or a private school to springboard her into the ivy league.

Nurse Lori was filling a vase at the bathroom sink as Hannah approached. A small pile of red and white lilies lay on the counter beside her scissors, cleanly snipped and ready for fresh water.

"I thought they were pretty," Nurse Lori said, nodding to the flowers. "You know, for this time of year."

"Yes, of course," Hannah agreed.

The blooms really were a perfect balance between classic and merriment. Just like Mr. Pringle. A ruthless businessman with little moral rectitude in the professional world... yet, soft enough that she'd catch his subtle tears watching the young ones on the playground.

"How are things at the school?"

Nurse Lori always asked after the children.

"Wonderful. Really great." Hannah hesitated. "Everyone has gotten used to Mr. Pringle's absence this year, but I think we all feel it more around the holidays."

"I understand, dear," Nurse Lori replied, dropping the flowers one by one into the vase. "It's so good of you to keep his dreams alive for the students."

"I couldn't give up on them if I tried," Hannah said. "I *was* them, not so long ago. I would've killed for opportunities like the ones Mr. Pringle provides for them."

"He is a good man," agreed Nurse Lori. "You can go inside whenever you're ready. It really is so kind of you to visit."

"He's done so much for me. I only wish I could do more."

She stepped into the dimly lit room where Mr. Pringle slept, snores escaping the thick bedcovers. Hannah stood above him, regretful of his condition, remembering how he chastised her years earlier for sleeping past nine. *The early bird gets the worm, Hannah. Don't you know?* She smiled at the memory, then frowned at the darkness.

He wasn't dead, for goodness sake. Not yet, anyway.

Hannah moved to the windows, pulling the string to open the curtains. Sunlight flooded the room, falling across the carpet in sharp triangular angles. It caught on the medicine cabinet, drawing her eye to the vials of medicines and chemicals, and then to the glassware sitting dusty on the bar in the corner.

Mr. Pringle grunted in his sleep but otherwise did not

react.

Hannah sighed as she stared out the window. The grounds extended far into the distance, dotted by wooded areas and gardens, some still with colorful shrubbery despite the early winter. If she leaned to her left, she could just make out her Jeep parked in the pink gravel driveway.

Another car had arrived since she did, a Porsche with shiny black paint. She recognized it as belonging to Mr. Pringle's lawyer, Bart. He must also be visiting today. Hannah supposed this was typical of the holiday season, everyone visiting loved ones, even a man so disoriented that he'd never know they were there.

She should probably consider herself lucky that Mr. Pringle was sleeping, prone as he'd been to intense delusions in the early weeks of this strange, impossible illness. Shouting at people, scaring away nurse after nurse. It had been horrible to watch. His current, unconscious state was terrible, too, but in a simpler way.

"What a beautiful day!" Nurse Lori spoke from the doorway. "We never let in nearly enough sunshine."

"I thought the same," Hannah replied, watching the nurse place lilies atop Mr. Pringle's dresser. "Those look nice there."

"Thank you," Nurse Lori said. "I wish he could enjoy them."

They both glanced at Mr. Pringle, still unmoving in bed.

"Does he sleep like this all day?"

"Yes," the nurse replied. "Dr. Luge asked me to provide a

sedative twice daily. To keep him comfortable, you know?"

"Sure," Hannah said, suddenly overcome by emotion at the thought. The formidable Chris Pringle, the kindest man she'd ever known, unfailingly generous, provider for children, an unstoppable force... Well, he hadn't been unstoppable at all. He'd been stopped short, actually, slammed so abruptly by this sickness and reduced to a sedated shell of what he'd been, unable even to leave his bed.

A tear slid down her cheek.

"I'm sorry, Nurse Lori. I have somewhere to be."

"Of course, Hannah." Nurse Lori smiled sadly at her. Hannah could tell the woman knew she was lying, but also thought she knew why. "Be well. And have a wonderful holiday."

Hannah hurried from the room, head bowed and ashamed of herself for leaving, but unable to stay. It was too much. She needed air. She was nearly three-quarters of the way down the hall when she froze, hearing Mrs. Pringle's voice around the corner.

"One hundred kisses for you! Thank you!"

Instinctively, Hannah snapped against the wall, sliding carefully and quietly to the very edge of the bend. She peeked around the side to see Mrs. Pringle kissing Bart on the cheek. Mr. Pringle's lawyer looked embarrassed at the gesture, stepping away.

"It was nothing, Mrs. Pringle. Absolutely nothing. Just my job."

"It was *everything*, Mr. Hansen."

"Well, then. I'll take these back to the office right away." He patted his briefcase. "You should keep the copies I left in the library for your records."

"I'll file them away for safekeeping," she assured him.

"Have a wonderful holiday, Mindy."

And with that, Bart disappeared down the hall, Mrs. Pringle watching him go. As soon as he was out of sight, she leaped into the air, nearly toppling over her heels. She whooped happily, then proceeded down the hall towards her bedroom.

Hannah turned the corner and approached the library. What could be inside to make Mrs. Pringle so happy? She'd seemed nothing but bitter and nasty every time Hannah spoke to her, though she knew that was probably because Mrs. Pringle did not like just how much money Mr. Pringle funneled into the school.

Evil woman.

Before she could convince herself otherwise, Hannah slipped into the library. In the center of the room, a stack of papers sat innocently on a large, round table beside a pack of Mrs. Pringle's smelly cigarettes. Hannah rushed to the paperwork, checking over her shoulder to make sure her detour remained unnoticed by any nearby staff.

She quickly scanned the top page.

Mindy,

As per our discussion, please find the following documents included in this package:

- Power of Attorney listing you as the agent for Mr. Chris Pringle

- Mr. Chris Pringle's updated Will and Testament

Thank you for completing the paperwork on behalf of your husband. I know Chris will rest easy knowing that both you and the school will be well cared for after his passing.

Please reach out with any questions.

Bart

Hannah's heart pounded as she reached the end of the cover letter. Mrs. Pringle had finally managed to update her husband's estate, something she'd been unsuccessfully attempting for nearly a decade. The woman never liked Mr. Pringle's decision to leave most of his wealth to the school.

Hannah tasted dirt as she thought of Mrs. Pringle celebrating in the hallway. Her boss' horrible wife felt entitled to the entire Pringle fortune as if *she* were the one who earned it, as if *she* built one of the most successful technology companies in history from the ground up. But she hadn't even been around in the early days. No, Mr. Pringle did it all on his own.

All *Mindy* did was marry him.

Hannah remembered Mr. Pringle entering her office, nearly giddy with excitement.

"Hannah! My arrangements are finalized, and I finally have some excellent news to share with you!" He'd bounced on the soles of his feet.

"What is it, Mr. Pringle?"

"Now, don't go wishing death on me, Hannah! But I've decided to leave everything to the school. The grounds, the money, all of it! It's best spent for the children here once I'm gone."

"All of it?" Hannah was stunned. "What about Mrs. Pringle?"

"Oh, I've set aside enough for her to live comfortably for many years, possibly the rest of her life if she manages the money well. Bart will help her."

"Are you sure about this?"

"Never been more sure about anything! Now toast with me, will you?!"

And he'd pulled a bottle of champagne from inside his coat. They spent the rest of the meeting dreaming of all the different ways the children could use the grounds and joking about Mr. Pringle outliving them all.

At the time, she'd thought of his death as something abstract, so far into the future that it wasn't real. They could laugh so easily about it. And then, one day when the time came, they'd simply dot the i's and cross the t's to give the students new facilities and more funding than they'd ever imagined.

She'd been so naïve.

With another quick glance at the library door, Hannah shuffled through the paperwork, muttering under her breath. Finally, she found it: Bart's summary of changes made to Mr. Pringle's final wishes. Something hot and unpleasant boiled in her gut as she read the words typed across the page, so carelessly dashing the hopes and dreams of thousands of kids.

That *evil*, gold-digging woman. Hannah bristled as she replaced the papers, striding back to the hallway. Her mind reeled with what Mrs. Pringle had done, with the loss of the inheritance that would have meant so much to so many. An image of Mrs. Pringle blossomed in her mind, her tall, skinny frame drowning in furs and jewelry. It was a disgusting contrast to the sick, frail man lying in bed down the hall.

It still didn't seem real. One day he was tossing a baseball with the students, and the next... It all happened so quickly. So unexpectedly, after years of health and mental acuity, even into his older years. How terrible it had been for Mr. Pringle to fall ill, and with something so strange and impossible to cure.

But then again... how absolutely convenient it all was for his wife. The thought echoed in her mind: How absolutely *convenient* for his Mindy Pringle.

Hannah thought she might be sick.

She stopped short, turning back towards Mr. Pringle's bedroom. That woman wouldn't get away with this. Not if Hannah had anything to say about it.

AMY GREEN

December 23
8:30 PM

Amy paced back and forth in the auction house office, talking herself off the cliff. She'd had the day from hell, and despite the hour, it wasn't nearly over yet.

Tonight was the annual Santa's Workshop Holiday Auction, one of the largest events of the year. The premise was simple: A massive silent auction of the finest donations from the gallery's biggest artists and clients, followed by a live auction of five extra-special pieces. All funded by Mr. Chris Pringle, with proceeds reserved for the Cove Harbor School for Excellence.

Amy spent the last year lining up artwork and planning the event. It was a prestigious honor to curate such an auction, both for her and for the gallery. She'd handled the past seven Holiday Auctions, each more successful than the last, but this year was different. This year, Mindy sought a new curator for the summer auction as well. And Amy was officially in the running.

Everything had to be perfect. And so it was, until last night.

Amy was the last to leave, predictably so for a dedicated employee with nobody to go home to, lingering well into the evening for one final check of the space. She walked the floor, arranging tablets in front of each auction lot and stopping to enjoy a few before they left for their new homes. She dusted off the decorations and sprinkled red and gold glitter over the white tablecloths, adjusting the garland and holiday lights until they were absolutely perfect.

Finally, she made her way to the back room where the live auction pieces awaited their fate, each chosen for their quality and seasonal charm. Her favorite was a medium-sized oil painting, a still life of a simple Christmas ornament resting on a Jacobean wood surface. It invoked a sense of light that took her breath away, not to mention its spectacular embrace of the holiday theme.

For a few minutes, she stood and stared at the painting, raking her eyes over the beautiful imagery. But then... she noticed something. Something that was just a little bit off. Unable to shake the sensation, Amy withdrew her phone from her back pocket and opened her photo gallery.

She swiped until she found an image she'd taken when she'd moved this painting out of storage last week. She raised the image on her phone to study it beside the one hanging on the auction house wall. At first, she saw no differences between the two paintings. They were perfectly, flawlessly identical. Until she saw the disparity.

It was so small. So seemingly insignificant, yet obvious once she'd spotted it.

The artist's signature was ever so slightly higher on the piece in front of her than it was in the image on her screen. Her heart raced as she rushed to the auction house office, searching frantically for a magnifying glass. Once she found one, a closer study of the painting caused her to recoil in horror, jerking away from the canvas.

There were more than enough red flags in the work for her to pull the piece for authentication. Of course, she'd already had each piece examined, and it passed without issue. But now... She couldn't ignore the misplaced signature. And the texture felt wrong, the brush strokes not quite matching the images beneath. There was too much evidence that this painting, one of the five pieces of honor, might actually be a fake.

A fake. In her auction. At the biggest event of her career.

She'd rushed back to the office, throwing the magnifying glass back in its drawer beneath shelves of preservation chemicals. Amy had wanted to tear her hair out. And now, back in the same office one day later, she wanted to do just the same.

Amy hadn't said anything about the potential counterfeit. She knew she should report it, but she also knew that doing so could be the end of her career. Or at least the end of her role in the Pringle benefits. She couldn't bring herself to throw it all away after she'd worked so hard. And how could she have seen this coming? She'd had every piece authenticated and appraised. She never cut corners. None of this made any sense.

After twenty-four hours of panicking, pacing, and driving herself crazy, she'd come to one conclusion. If the painting *was* a fraud, it must have been switched with the real one after she removed it from storage hardly a week ago. But how could that be? Nobody had access to the art other than those directly involved in the benefit. It just didn't make sense.

Amy squeezed her eyes shut tight, pressing a palm to her forehead. She'd made her decision last night when she declined to report the potential crime. For better or worse, she had no choice but to continue with the auction. They were just thirty minutes from the start of the live event, and Amy needed to be present.

She braced herself and stepped through the door.

The bustle of the busy crowd, usually music to her organizer ears, now only heightened her anxiety. Which one of these bidders would win the painting? Which would take home a potential counterfeit? Would they know? Would they ever find out? She couldn't dwell on it.

Jingle Bell Rock played as she drummed her fingers on her thigh, restless and shaky, forcing herself to walk the room. Carl, the auction house owner, did the same nearby, greeting clientele and calling their attention to various pieces of artwork in the silent auction. The live event would begin shortly, bringing with it a likely flood of bidders on the suspected forgery.

Amy surveyed the party, noting the usual attendees and familiar faces of Cove Harbor's art scene, as well as some here just for this event. The heavyset doctor rumored to have an extraordinary private collection sipped wine with a local artist near the podium, while a brunette woman with a Cove Harbor School bracelet spoke quietly to a tall man who worked for Mr. Pringle, the worry on their faces matching her own.

Across the room, Mindy Pringle sipped her wine, laughing delicately with a lady clad in a gaudy ruby necklace. Cocktail waitresses circled the room with platters of champagne and every miniature holiday hors d'oeuvre the caterer could devise. On the surface, it was a lovely party. Amy should be proud.

She swallowed as Mindy bade goodbye to her friend and started toward her. After seven years, Mindy was a friend as well as her boss, often joining her for a weekend lunch or Friday night cocktails. Now she sauntered over, followed by the faint scents of perfume, wine, and stale cigarette smoke.

"Good evening, Mindy. How are you enjoying the event?"

"It's just brilliant, Amy. The artwork looks even more fabulous than it did at the viewing. I actually think I might bid on one of the live pieces."

"Really?" Amy's throat felt raw and scratchy. "Which one?"

"Well, I just love that painting with the Christmas ornament. But I think I have my sights set on the sculpture of the angels. There's something hauntingly beautiful about them. Don't you agree?"

"Oh, yes... Of course." Relief dulled some of Amy's nerves. "We were lucky to receive such beautiful holiday-themed pieces this year. I actually think -" But Mindy was no longer listening.

"Excuse me a moment, will you?" Mindy stepped around Amy, staring at something over her shoulder. Or someone, rather. Amy followed Mindy's gaze to a shockingly handsome man who'd just arrived, standing tall and smiling at Mindy. Mindy, however, appeared positively furious to see him there.

Amy followed behind, concerned.

"What do you think you're doing here?" Mindy growled at the man, who continued to smile back at her, one hand lifting to Mindy's minuscule waist. "Do you want to be found out?" She swatted his hand away.

Amy flushed hot around the collar, realizing at once that this man was intimately involved with Mindy. She shouldn't be surprised, really, what with the age difference between Mindy and Mr. Pringle. And especially now, as Mr. Pringle had been incapacitated by illness for so long.

Still, she couldn't help a twinge of jealousy. It had been so long since anyone placed a hand on *her* waist like that. And that stranger was so handsome, she could almost feel him from here, almost imagine the feel of his hands – Amy blushed, realizing she was staring too long, lingering awkwardly. They'd think she was eavesdropping, though she'd hardly taken in a word they'd said.

She quickly stepped away, nearly colliding with another man.

"Ms. Green?"

"Yes?" Dave, her account manager at Cove Harbor bank, stood before her. "Oh, hello. I didn't realize you'd be here."

"I'm representing the bank. We are avid supporters of Chris Pringle and his school. We even offer two internships annually to the students." Dave smiled. "I'm glad to see you. I've been attempting to reach you all day. Did you see my email?"

"Sorry – I didn't see it. I'm the curator for the auction, so it's been a crazy day."

"Yes, I thought that might be the case." Dave sipped his red wine. "Anyway, we had a little problem with the transfer into your account. Every so often, large deposits like yours will trigger a security check in our system. It won't take long to fix. Can you come in after the holiday to get it sorted out?"

"Hang on..." Amy said. "What deposit? My paychecks don't clear until the end of the month."

"Your paychecks?" Dave stared at her like she was insane. "I was referring to your other account."

"I'm sorry – I'm confused. What other account? I only have one."

"You're hilarious, Amy. A real riot." Dave chuckled. "I've

always liked that about you, even though I don't always understand your sense of humor."

"I'm not kidding, Dave." She put her hand on her hip. "I have no idea what you're talking about."

"Well, here... I can pull up the email I sent you earlier." Dave withdrew his phone and opened an email with an attached statement. "Let's look at it together."

Dave angled the phone towards her, revealing a bank statement with her name at the top. *Amy Green.* That was her... But there was no way in hell that this was her account. The statement showed a series of deposits totaling nearly five hundred thousand dollars.

Then she saw the balance.

Wow. Definitely *not* her account.

"Dave. This is not my account. It must be a different Amy Green."

"You are the only Amy Green in Cove Harbor. Trust me, I would know."

"Trust *me!*" Amy was getting frustrated. "If I had that kind of money, do you think I'd be living in a one-bedroom apartment over Reels?" The restaurant had good food and all, but that was about the only decent reason to rent the place above it.

She looked at the email address on Dave's phone. *amygreen@potmail.com.*

"Potmail? Who uses Potmail? I'm Amy M Green at Bmail, like every other self-respecting millennial. That other email address is not mine!"

Anxiety ached in her stomach as every alarm in her brain blared simultaneously. For the second time in the past twenty-four hours, her intuition screamed at her. Something wasn't right. Something wasn't right at all.

"Dave, I need to know when and how this account was set up. I'm telling you, it's not mine. I have no idea where it came from."

Dave looked worried now, too.

"But... if it's not yours, who's is it?"

"I don't have any idea."

"Okay..." Dave said slowly. "Come to the bank tomorrow before we close for the holiday. I'll meet you there, and we'll figure this out."

"Alright," she replied. It wasn't exactly how she wanted to spend her Christmas Eve, but at least it might take her mind off the ornament painting.

Dave strode away, likely seeking less-dramatic conversation, leaving Amy staring after him as he joined the woman from Cove Harbor school and her companion. They hardly smiled as he approached, and she again noticed their concerned demeanors, but didn't dwell on it. She had enough of her own problems to worry about.

Amy turned away then nearly jumped out of her skin.

"Hey!" She faltered, her voice catching, face just inches from someone else's. It was the handsome man she'd seen Mindy argue with earlier. His eyes were so blue, like the underside of glaciers she'd seen only in photographs, even more captivating up close.

"Walk with me?"

"Sure," she stammered, following him to the auction house office.

Her mind accelerated into fantasies of this good-looking stranger, the first to pay her any attention since her last relationship ended nearly a year ago. He closed the door behind them, and she found herself backed up against the bookshelf, staring upward as he leaned over her, one arm resting above her head.

She thought she might faint.

All thoughts of fraudulent paintings and the Pringle benefit were driven from her mind as she took in the moment. It'd been so long since she had chemistry like this with anyone. Who cared if he was seeing Mindy? He lowered his eyes to hers and she almost closed them in anticipation.

But then he spoke.

"I need you to tell Dave that the account is yours."

"Excuse me?" Amy squeaked. "Who are you? Were you eavesdropping?"

"It's not important. But I promise, you'll save us both a world of trouble if you confirm the account belongs to you."

"What trouble?" Amy ducked out from under his arm. She felt as though she'd lost track of something important, like the train was flying off the rails but she was still standing alone at the station, wishing she was on board to pull the brake.

"Trust me, Amy. Failing to do as I ask will lead only to

your arrest for the worst art fraud in Cove Harbor history."

He smiled at her.

"Art fraud? You mean..."

The door flung open, crashing into a filing cabinet, and Mindy stepped inside.

"Mindy!" Amy said, relieved. "Your boyfriend was just telling me..."

"He's *not* my boyfriend, Amy." Mindy rolled her eyes. "Don't be stupid." Then she turned to the man. "You're too much of an idiot to be my boyfriend."

The man put his hand over his heart in mock injury. "Ouch."

"Shut up!" Mindy snapped. "You had one job! Just one! Make the counterfeit. Not tell the goddamned art curator about it."

"Hang on..." Amy said. "You were the one? You swapped the paintings?"

"Amy, so help me," Mindy snarled. "You will go to that bank tomorrow and tell them that the account belongs to you. And then I don't want to hear another word about it."

"But Mindy... That's not my account."

"*But Mindy, that's not my account.*" Mindy mocked in a voice that sounded nothing like Amy's. "Save yourself the drama, Amy, and tell them that it is. Otherwise, you'll have bigger problems than some bank error."

"But I didn't do anything wrong!"

"Of course you did! Otherwise, where did you get all that money?"

Amy's head spun like she was falling, untethered, through space.

"It is *you* who's been receiving mysterious deposits since you began curating the auction. It's *your* name on the phone used to arrange the swaps. And it's only *your* email address that's consistently logged into every art auction site on the dark web for the past seven years."

Amy opened her mouth, but she seemed to have lost her voice. She gaped at Mindy.

"So, now, I'll remind you. Any investigation of fraud at this auction will reveal just one guilty party. So tomorrow morning, you're going to walk into that bank and own the account. You're in it now, Amy, and there's no way out."

And with that, Mindy turned, stepping through the office door. The handsome man flashed her an apologetic smile before following, leaving Amy leaning against the bookshelf of chemicals and preservation handbooks for support.

She didn't cry. She didn't sink to her knees, or fall to the ground in a heap. She took a moment to let it all wash over her. The knowledge of what Mindy had done was so colossal that it seemed to grow unrestricted, filling the room and threatening to drown her if she didn't escape, didn't run for her life.

Amy stumbled through the door, nearly colliding with a cocktail waitress as she emerged into the event. The young woman righted her tray, the liquid in the champagne glasses wobbling, and glared at Amy. She opened her mouth to apologize to the server, but then –

"Thank you, thank you," Mindy's amplified voice filled the room. "Thank you for attending this benefit. If only my dear husband Chris could be here to see you fill the room in support of his wonderful school."

Mindy's voice trailed away, drowned by the sound of raging waves, piling atop one another until she heard nothing but their rush and tumble. Awash with indignant fury, Amy whipped out her phone, typing a text to Mindy.

> Mindy. You're right. Please meet me for coffee tomorrow so we can discuss what I need to tell the bank.

Then she opened a new email, this one to someone she hardly knew, but who could undoubtedly help her. She pressed send with an uncharacteristic vengeance, stabbing her finger into the button with a sense of purpose she hoped she wouldn't regret.

CHRISTOPHER PRINGLE

December 24
3:30 AM

Chris swallowed a lump in his throat the size of Manhattan. He tried to speak, but couldn't, his throat raw with disuse. His legs moved beneath the blanket, weak and frail before he finally propped himself up on his elbows, squinting into the dark room.

"Hello?" It came out like a whisper. Oh, hell.

He struggled past the pounding, deafening pain in his head. It felt like he'd drank an entire bottle of whiskey, like the worst hangover of his life magnified by one hundred, hopped up twentyfold, and then injected with steroids.

What was happening to him?

Chris dragged his feet over the edge of the mattress, grabbing the bedpost for support. He yanked a blood pressure strap off his bicep and pulled monitoring wires from his body. Slowly, carefully, he tested his weight. His head spun, but after a moment, he steadied himself on his feet. Then he shuffled, one foot in front of the other, towards the bathroom.

Before he reached the doorway, however, Chris noticed a small piece of yellow paper tucked into the glassware on his bar. He recognized it immediately as the school's office stationery and changed course, slowly inching across the room to retrieve it. His name was printed neatly across the fold, blurry in his vision.

"Damnit," he croaked, now hobbling back to the nightstand for his glasses. Finally able to see, he unfolded the paper, flipping on his bedside lamp.

Mr. Pringle,

I don't know if this is my place, but as your friend and longtime colleague, I feel obliged to leave you this note. Even if I did not work for the school, I would still write this letter. I know how important the children are to you.

Mindy has taken power of attorney over your estate and changed your will. The school is no longer slated to receive what you intended, unless she dies before you. She was gracious enough to allow us to keep your inheritance in the oh-so-terrible instance of her death. Hope it happens soon. Just kidding.

In all seriousness, I don't know what to do other than leave you this letter. I've spoken to your nurse, and I think she agrees with me that there is something fishy going on here. In the event that she follows through on withholding your sedative and you wake up this evening, please know that I'm committed to doing everything in my power to support you.

Here's hoping you actually read this,
Hannah

Chris read the letter three times to make sense of it. Mindy changed his will? How could she have done that so quickly? And why on Earth would Bart help her obtain power of attorney? His eyes lingered on a new cabinet beside his bookshelf, and he made his way over to it. A peek inside the glass doors told him it was a medicine cabinet, filled to the brim with every substance imaginable.

He closed his eyes, the pounding still thundering in his ears. He tried to silence it, but to no avail, everything humming with the powerful writhing in his skull. He wandered to the glowing screen Mindy placed on the bookshelf when she'd had the speakers installed. It was one of those annoying assistant devices that everyone swore by, though he hardly used it for much beyond requesting the weather forecast.

Chris' eyes found the little white numbers glowing in the upper corner above the date, and he did a double take.

December?! Impossible. It couldn't be December!

"What's going on here!?" Chris shouted, though it came out quiet as a mouse. "Hello?!" He strode to the window, whipping back the curtains. A light flurry descended on the other side of the glass. *Snow.* Holy shit. It really was December. He'd been so certain it was July.

"Mr. Pringle?!"

"Nurse Lori?" The woman entered the room uncertainly. "What's going on here?! How can it be December...?"

Nurse Lori was at his side in an instant, extending her arm for him to lean on.

"Mr. Pringle... You're up, on your feet. Hannah said... But I never really thought..."

"Please," The word felt pathetic spoken in this tone he'd never used before. "Tell me what's going on." It couldn't be December. Summer had hardly started.

Nurse Lori helped him ease onto the bed. He hated the relief he felt at being off his feet, but couldn't help the sigh that escaped as his bottom hit the bedspread.

"Thank you." He smiled at her through his confusion. "Now, will you please explain what is happening to me?"

"I'm not really sure, Mr. Pringle." Nurse Lori looked uncomfortable now. "Hannah came to see you today, as she does most weeks. She rushed out suddenly... Seemed upset. Then she came flying back in with a crazy story."

Chris had trouble imagining the scene. It wasn't like Hannah to overreact, to panic in stressful moments. She was a level-headed, practical young woman who thrived under pressure. He'd never once seen her lose her composure, despite the many difficult situations they'd encountered over the past ten years.

"What exactly did Hannah say?"

"She said that your wife... Well, that your wife was dishonest. That she'd somehow fooled your attorney into giving her control over your estate, and she'd changed your will. And then..." Nurse Lori hesitated.

"And then, what? What else?"

"And then... And then she said that she was suspicious of your illness. See, Mr. Pringle, you've been laid up for months. Dr. Luge has been tending to you, and I've helped of course, and two other nurses who I rotate shifts with. Hannah thought something seemed strange about your illness, and when she found the paperwork showing Mrs. Pringle had adjusted your will... Well, she jumped to a few conclusions."

"If I've been sick for months, why am I better now?"

"I don't know that you are. Hannah asked me about your condition, and I told her everything I knew. In the beginning, you were having, well..." She looked away from him. "Delusions. Shouting, going on about things that weren't real. Fabrications. But recently, your vitals have sometimes stabilized. I told her that there are days you seem nearly healthy, but then you decline again." Nurse Lori stared at her hands. "We give you a sedative twice a day on Dr. Luge's orders. At six in the morning and six at night. To keep you comfortable."

"Comfortable?"

"Yes, and to help with the pain."

"If you've been shooting me up with sedatives, why am I awake?"

"Hannah said..." Nurse Lori trembled with anxiety. "Hannah said we would never get to the bottom of this if you stayed asleep in your bed. She asked me to skip your sedative tonight. To see what happens."

"Well, surprise, Nurse Lori. I'm awake." His voice sounded bitter, but at least it was stronger now.

"How are you feeling?"

"My head is fucking ringing. But otherwise, I feel fine. Weak," He added. "But I'm no spring chicken."

Nurse Lori chuckled, her eyes darting from side to side.

"You said Dr. Luge has been looking after me?"

"Yes. Since the summer."

"He's the art collector, right? The one with the premises down near the water?"

"That's the one."

"Well, I think we'd better call him."

Nurse Lori nodded, hurrying from the room.

Chris remained seated on the bed for another moment. He was disoriented, nearly incapacitated by the aching headache. But he wouldn't rest until he figured out what was happening. He thought of Mindy. No wonder the woman married him. His buddies were right... She was too young, too beautiful to be after anything *but* his money.

But even if there had been doubts, he never imagined

she'd go this far. How could she be so heartless? Steal from the school? All those children... He'd have to talk to Bart about a divorce. And while he's at it, maybe he should buy the man something nice. He may have helped Mindy change his will, but it was also he who convinced Chris to arrange a prenup to begin with.

Chris leaned back in his pillows, willing his head to stop throbbing. He tried closing his eyes, then holding his breath. He drained a glass of water Nurse Lori brought for him. He lowered the brightness of his bedside lamp, and even squeezed the pressure points he'd learned from his acupressure therapist. But to no avail. His head continued to pound like a bass drum at the Memorial Day Parade.

Finally, he rose from his bed and collected his walking cane from its hook in the closet. He leaned against it, shuffling down the hall until he reached his office. Chris settled into his enormous leather chair, the one he chose for its high back that reminded him of the tycoons he idolized as a child. His fingers brushed the computer mouse in front of him, and the screen came to life.

Reflexively, he opened his email, horrified at the thousands of messages left unanswered over the past six months. Despite the overwhelm, his fingers itched to open them, to get back to work. He'd always been a workaholic. But, then again, weren't most successful people? Chris never begrudged his drive to do more, not after all he'd achieved in his life.

He opened the first email in his inbox, received just hours

earlier. It took a moment for him to place the sender's name behind the pounding in his temples.

Amy Green, the art curator.

Mr. Pringle,

I hope this email finds you well, or finds you at all. I understand you've been too sick to play an active role in this year's Santa's Workshop Holiday Auction, but I've come across information that you should know.

Your wife, Ms. Mindy Pringle, has become involved in an illegal art trade. It appears that she's swapped out original pieces, replacing them with counterfeits. I believe she's been doing this for years, though I've only just realized yesterday.

Mindy has threatened to frame me for her crimes. Reaching out to you is my hail mary thrown in the final minutes of the game. I've always heard of your dedication to the Cove Harbor School for Excellence, and I hope that you remember I've always served the school as best I could in curating your benefits.

Please help me clear my name.

Thank you,
Amy Green

The pounding in Chris' head now surpassed anything he'd ever felt in his life. Everything felt watery, moving at the edges of his vision. He re-read Amy's email, grasping at his thoughts before they slipped through the cracks, lost in the pain. It didn't make sense. Why would Mindy steal art? She had no appreciation for the fine arts, never had.

"Mr. Pringle?" Nurse Lori appeared in the doorway. "The doctor is here."

"Coming, coming," Chris replied. His thoughts continued crawling, slowly marching through his consciousness. Even if Mindy wanted her own art collection, couldn't she have simply purchased some for herself? She wouldn't know the difference between the most priceless pieces and the mass-produced garbage she could find at the home goods store. And what did any of this have to do with his will? Could it be connected?

He entered his quarters to find Dr. Luge seated on his couch.

"Mr. Pringle!" the man sputtered. "How – Well, isn't this just wonderful to see you out of bed!" But his eyes shot towards the ceiling above Chris' shoulder as he said it. And something clicked into place so solidly in Chris' brain, he thought he almost heard it through the haze of his migraine.

And Mr. Pringle smiled.

"Dr. Luge," he said slowly. "What illness has befallen me? What has caused so much pain that I must be sedated, bedridden for months, with no end in sight?"

Dr. Luge stuttered.

"What, exactly," Chris stood taller now, pushing himself to his full height. "has been *so painful* as to warrant this?!"

Dr. Luge opened his mouth to answer, but Chris raised a hand.

"Save it," Chris growled, glaring at the other man. "I don't know what my wife would want with fine art... But I've heard of your *Noir* gallery, your secret chambers. Yes, I know exactly what *you* would want with it. I think you two have been scheming together."

"Mr. Pringle," Dr. Luge said, regaining his composure. "I'm sorry to say that your illness has the unfortunate side effects of delusions. You appear to be suffering from them now."

"I am *not* having delusions," Chris said, raising his voice. "I am not!"

He needed to find a phone, to call someone, anyone, before this man loaded him up with sedatives again. Chris turned abruptly, leaving the room, his cane clomping along beside him. He slammed it into the ground, the noise muted by the carpet.

Dr. Luge followed him down the hall and around the corner to the library, but he did not attempt to stop him. Chris strode through the high-ceilinged room, past the stack of paper and Mindy's cigarettes, and to the phone at the other end of the hall.

He picked up the phone, but then...

"Stop," Dr. Luge said. "You can call whoever you want, but

they will tell you the same thing that I did. You are having delusions!" The doctor strode towards the table, picking up the top sheet on the stack and lowering·his voice. The moonlight illuminated the scar on his hand. "Mindy has power of attorney. A court has already deemed you medically unfit on the basis of your illness and delusions."

Chris hesitated, still holding the phone in the air.

"It won't do you any good, Mr. Pringle. I'm telling you the truth. You must know I am! You're acting crazy. And don't you feel ill? Put down the phone and return to bed."

Chris lowered the phone, his eyes trailing from the paper in the doctor's hand to the cigarettes on the table. *Curse, Mindy*, he thought. *Curse her to hell.* His head pounded rhythmically.

"Now, that's a good man," said Dr. Luge. Chris clenched his fists, nails biting into his palms. "Come now, back to bed."

Chris followed the doctor back to his quarters. But Chris Pringle was no fool. You didn't make it as far as he had in life by being foolish. Or by being a pushover who fell to other people's whims, bending and breaking under the pressure.

He kept his head, remaining calm and perfectly collected all the way back to his quarters, past the medicine cabinet, and right into bed. Then he lay down, confessed to his delusions, and thanked the good doctor for coming to his aid in the middle of the night.

He lay quietly and waited, waited for the doctor to leave

and his nurse to retire to her nearby bedroom. For he treated Nurse Lori to a subtle wink behind Dr. Luge's back, and though he may be sedated now, he trusted that he wouldn't be for much longer. She trusted him, and he was grateful for that.

For when all was quiet, Chris Pringle had something very important to do.

AN AUTOPSY

December 28
12:00 PM

Dr. Darcy puzzled over the cold steel table. Mindy Pringle's body lay before her, sporting all the signs of a nearly completed autopsy, an incision visible in her torso. Samples from the exam littered the tabletops, interspersed with lab reports and other evidence unearthed by the Cove Harbor Police Force.

The cause of death was obvious. Mindy had been poisoned.

Yet... Dr. Darcy was stumped. Mindy's hot chocolate, initially believed to be the source of the peril, was clean of any nefarious substances.

Dr. Darcy rested her chin in her hands, deep in thought.

~

Miles away, Mr. Chris Pringle sipped his coffee. He'd spent most of the night catching up on emails and sifting through his company's records from the past few months. Harry collected every report he could, having them all printed, bound, and added to the pile waiting on his desk each morning.

He didn't miss Mindy. Not in the slightest. Good riddance, he thought, as he replied to an email from Hannah. The young woman had been overjoyed to hear from him but not as happy as she was when Mindy collapsed at the coffee shop.

He couldn't blame her. Hannah devoted her life to the school and desperately wanted reassurance that the children would receive what he'd promised from his estate. Little did she know, a very apologetic Bart was working on yet another adjustment to the will at this very moment.

Chris might not have children of his own, but Hannah was as close as could be, and she deserved to be remembered in his estate, too. In that spirit, he'd asked Bart to allocate Mindy's original share to Hannah. It would be enough for her to live well after he was gone. Though, as his new doctor confirmed, that likely wouldn't be for quite some time.

~

Dr. Darcy again reviewed the analysis report from the hot chocolate. The beverage had not tested positive for any known poisons. She'd even checked for lesser-known natural toxins, like poisonous plants, and any innocuous substance she could think of that became harmful in high amounts.

She'd found clear evidence of arsenic in the woman's blood. But how did it get there? She wandered across the exam room, lifting a small glass vial from its place on the table. Absently, she collected her zinc and acid, preparing yet another test for the presence of arsenic.

~

Dr. Luge sat in a small, square cell, kicking the floor with his feet. He cursed Mr. Chris Pringle for landing him here. This was all Mindy's fault, anyway. How could she have been so stupid as to let *anyone,* especially some busybody protegee of her idiot husband, find out that she'd altered his will?

All they'd needed was one more week. One more week to distribute that final, fatal dose. One more week and he'd have been home free, receiving forbidden originals from every Pringle benefit from now until the end of time. He'd have the most elaborate black-market gallery in this part of the world, and all in exchange for the simple act of keeping Mr. Chris Pringle sick, sedated, and out of his wife's way.

One more week. That was all he would've needed.

~

Dr. Darcy's nose was inches from the witness reports. The barista made the hot chocolate. Mindy's friend Amy picked it up from the counter. Mindy came inside, then drank from the cup, and collapsed. Dr. Darcy already ruled out the hot chocolate and the cup, neither of which contained any trace of the poison.

She read it again, carefully poring over Amy Green's statement. Then she hurried to her phone, dialing the police station.

"Chief Williams?"

"Hi, Dr. Darcy. How can I help?"

"I think I've just realized something about the Mindy Pringle case."

"Excellent. I'm all ears."

"Do you know what happened to Mindy's cigarette?"

~

A woman sat alone at Reels, scrolling her phone as she bit into a french fry. She flicked her rubber bracelet further up her wrist, away from the ketchup pooled along the rim of her plate.

"Can I join you?"

Hannah's heart jumped as she looked up to see Harry standing over her.

"Sure," she said, patting the empty seat beside her.

"And can I buy you a drink?"

"It's the middle of the day," she said, laughing. "Although I suppose school is closed for a few more days."

"It's settled then. Champagne all around!"

"What are we celebrating?"

"The downfall of Meredith Blake."

She swatted his arm.

"That's terrible, Harry. Really. I mean, she *died.*"

Harry paused, then met her eyes.

"Let's celebrate something else then. Would you like to spend New Years with me?"

"You mean, like a date?"

"Yeah... Like a date."

And, as they say, the rest was history.

~

Chief Williams hurried into the autopsy room, an evidence bag clutched in his hands. Dr. Darcy jumped from her chair to meet him.

"They picked this up at the scene," Chief Williams said. "Let's see what you've got."

Dr. Darcy snapped on her latex gloves and pulled open the bag. She reached inside with her tweezers, carefully removing a partially smoked, half-crushed cigarette dotted with pink lipstick. She removed a small sample from the outer rim, dropping it carefully into a glass test tube.

Finally, she added her acid and zinc, sealing it closed.

~

"Amy?"

Amy shook herself, regaining her composure.

"Did you hear what I said?"

"Yes. Sorry, Dave. You said the money is no longer in the account?"

"That's right." The account manager looked nervous. "It's all gone. Everything was withdrawn yesterday."

"And is it possible to trace it?"

"We have people working on that," he said. "But I wouldn't waste your time worrying about it. After all, it wasn't your money, anyway, right?"

"I suppose not..." Amy furrowed her brow, then repeated, "I suppose not."

A thousand miles away, a man with very blue eyes lay on white sand, his hand inches from a paintbrush. An unfinished seaside scene decorated his canvas, while a bank card burned a hole in his pocket. He thought of the money sitting in his account, waiting to be spent, and he smiled.

Thank you, Amy Green.

~

Dr. Darcy held the glass test tube in the air.

"We're going to ignite the gas in this vial," she explained

to the Chief. "If arsenic is present on the sample from the cigarette, black marks will appear on this dish."

He nodded, and she lit the flame, holding up her white ceramic plate.

Their eyes met, satisfaction between them.

Deposits smeared the plate in Dr. Darcy's hand, as black as the coal of any chimney against freshly fallen snow, or as the heart of the woman lying cold on the table beside them.

~

Back at the Pringle manor, Chris tossed a final pack of Mindy's cigarettes in the trash. Smoking really was such a deadly habit.

MURDER IN THE MAIN OFFICE

BLOOD IN THE CARPET

March 31
6:25 AM

Kate's shoes clicked loudly against the checkerboard tile, each step echoing off the walls of lockers around her. It was the quiet before the morning storm of teenagers traipsed in from their cars and buses. They'd enter loudly and messily, mucking the neatly mopped floors and breaking the silence, all else forgotten as they greeted one another in this most careless of life's chapters.

"Anderson!"

Kate turned in surprise, catching her bag on the corner of a bulletin board overflowing with the midterm projects from a foreign language course. She made a face and unsuccessfully attempted to nudge the flap of a student-made brochure back into place. Shrugging, she turned to see her favorite Assistant Principal emerging from a stairwell behind her.

"Hey, Jenkins." Kate smiled at the other woman, hoping she hadn't noticed the disruption of the bulletin board.

"You're here early."

"Just prepping an exam for tomorrow. Can you believe this downpour?"

"You're telling me! Though I suppose it's just that time of year." AP Jenkins wiped a bead of sweat from her forehead. She was quite red in the face, Kate noticed, as Jenkins coughed slightly into her sleeve.

"Are you okay?" Kate rummaged in her pocket to offer a crumpled tissue. Jenkins accepted it with a grateful smile, dabbing first her mouth and then her brow.

"Oh, yes, thank you... It's just the heat in this building. Full blast, no moderation. You'd think we could invest in a better system, eh?" Jenkins chuckled, though Kate hardly heard humor in it.

Kate smiled hesitantly. She liked AP Jenkins but was never sure where the line fell between colleague, friend, and supervisor. After a moment, she decided not to join her in complaining about the heating system, especially as she felt perfectly comfortable on this particular morning. Jenkins dropped the tissue into the wide trash bin of an abandoned custodial cart as they passed.

"Looks like Gordon is here early, too," Kate said, nodding towards the cart.

"Gordon?"

"The custodian..."

"Oh, yes, of course. Gordon..."

Jenkins held open the door to the Main Office as Kate stepped inside, passed the reception counter, and entered the alcove of staff mailboxes. She reached hers in a few steps, withdrawing a small pile of papers. Atop the stack was a bright blue sheet with familiar bubbly handwriting dancing along the top margin.

Professional Development Training Session, it read, with Friday's date and *Kelly's* written beneath. She laughed, recognizing Cove Harbor's local dive bar. Just as she peered around to see how many other mailboxes received the same note, a scream pierced the stillness.

"ARGHH!"

"Hello!?" Kate shouted. Nobody answered, and she ran back to the Main Office, stopping short at the scene ahead. AP Jenkins stood with her hand clasped over her mouth, pointing in shock at something on the ground behind the reception counter. Kate rushed forward, heart pounding, then gasped, papers scattering to the floor.

There lay Principal Kirk, choppy haircut lost in the pool of blood around him. Though most of the dark red liquid had hardened into the Main Office's thick carpeting, it seemed to Kate as if it oozed endlessly from him, clashing horribly with the bright blue of the now-forgotten happy hour invitation.

ERIC HAYWOOD

March 30
9:30 AM

Eric's watch rumbled against his wrist as he opened his mouth to address the class. He clenched his fist, fighting the urge to peek at the flashing notification.

"Five more minutes, everyone!"

"Mr. Haywood!" A voice called from the back table. "I need help!"

"Coming, Jenny!" He kept his eyes away from his smartwatch. *Don't do it,* he told himself sternly. *Don't check it. Just ignore it. Now is not the time.* But in the end, he couldn't resist. Eric tapped the little screen, staring for just long enough to read the email subject line.

Tenure Decision.

He went hot and then cold. His stomach dropped.

"Mr. Haaaaaaaywood!"

"On my way, Jenny!" He hurried to the back of the room.

The next fifteen minutes of class dragged like the slowest sludge of mud oozing towards the gymnasium door on this rainy spring day. He willed the seconds to tick faster, reminding himself to keep smiling, talking, and helping the kids with their research projects.

Finally, after an eternity of a class period, the bell rang. Cove Harbor High did not use a shrill, loud bell like you'd hear in the movies. It was more like a beep, quietly reminding everyone it was time to move along. A tenth grader once told him it was a b note, but he'd never double-checked the pitch.

The students rose and filed out as they did every day this year, his sixth year teaching. Six years of long hours for little pay. Of coaching, volunteering, and spending every spare penny on whatever he needed to teach history to the kids of this little town. And it all culminated in the email he'd just received from the principal.

Tenure Decision.

He closed the door behind the last lingering student, a quirky senior named Bo who didn't always try his best but wasn't his biggest slacker, either.

"See you later, Mr. H!" Bo called behind him, hurrying to catch up with his friends down the hall. Eric couldn't help but crack a smile at the sight of them bouncing away, galivanting through the spring of their final year of high school. What would become of them? Only time could tell.

His anxiety returned with the click of the closing door, and he hurried to his computer, a screensaver undulating at his desk. He jabbed his finger at the enter key and the login screen came alive. Eric frantically typed in his password.

Incorrect password. Please try again.

He grumbled and entered it again, this time successfully. He clicked the blue icon on his toolbar, and his email popped up. The little circle spun and spun, Eric's unrest growing with each passing second. Then, the window dulled out.

"Son of a bitch!" he cried, cursing his ancient computer. He force-closed the app and restarted it. "Come on, come on, come on..."

And there it was, sitting at the top of his inbox.

Tenure Decision.

He took a deep breath, then opened the email.

> **From:** dmyers@coveharborschools.org
> **Subject:** Tenure Decision
>
> Dear Mr. Haywood,
>
> We regret to inform you that the district has declined to offer you tenure this school year. We value the expertise and positive results you bring to our community and would like to offer you another probationary year with Cove Harbor High School.
>
> If you should accept, you will be eligible for

tenure again next spring.

Attached, you will find a link to a shared folder with your observation results from the past six school years.

Please pay careful consideration to your two most recent observations, both of which played a significant role in our tenure decision. Each contains actionable steps for you to improve your ratings next school year.

Wishing you all the best,
Mrs. D. Myers
Superintendent
Cove Harbor Schools

Eric groaned, then cursed into the silent classroom. How could they extend his probation?! He worked night and day for this job, getting the juniors through their state exams and even talking the senioritis out of the school's most apathetic students.

How *dare* they?

He growled behind his teeth and clicked on the attached folder in the email. His last two observations... He hardly remembered them. Principal Kirk had postponed both debriefs for so long that they'd never actually met to discuss the results. Eric drummed his fingers on the table while he waited for the folder to load, then clicked the first observation in question.

Kirk rated him in a multiple areas, but one stood out in bright red font among the others.

2e. Organizing Physical Space: Ineffective.

"Ineffective?" Eric scratched his head. When had he ever been rated ineffective, the lowest of the four classifications, in anything? In all his years teaching, he'd never received any score below 'effective.' Hell, he was even accustomed to a respectable number of 'highly-effectives' in his observation reports.

He scrolled down to read Principal Kirk's notes in the full description.

> **2e. Organizing Physical Space- Ineffective**
> Teacher remained seated in front of students for the duration of the period. Teacher refused to leave his seat, despite student requests for help, addressing them only from his chair.
>
> Teacher instruction would have been more effective if accompanied by constant circulation around the room to assist students.
>
> Additionally, teacher arranged student desks in a horseshoe instead of the recommended groups this district believes fosters student growth and cooperative learning.

Eric was really confused now. When had he ever spent an entire class period sitting in the front of the room? He checked the date on the observation report. It was from November. He thought back to the fall.

Wait a minute...

Eric broke his ankle at the end of October. No shit, he was sitting down, he was wearing a cast! And he'd dragged himself in every day, balancing on his crutches through the fallen leaves and slick autumn sidewalks. He kicked himself for not checking his evaluation results earlier. Unbelievable! And now it would be too late to challenge the rating or file a grievance with the union.

He thought hard, remembering the day the principal observed him. The desks *had* been in a horseshoe, but only to allow him to roll his desk chair from student to student, instead of hobbling on those uncomfortable crutches. His armpits had been intensely sore even just a few days after his injury.

He remembered Kirk's presence in the room, but he didn't recall any commentary decrying the seating arrangement. The principal even joked about Eric's dedication and how impressed he was that he continued teaching with his broken ankle. Eric now burned with anger and frustration at the memory.

What the fuck was Kirk's problem?

Eric closed out the observation report and opened the next one. Dread swept over him as his eyes fell on the date. Just five weeks after the first observation. He still would've been in the cast.

"No way," he said to the empty room. "No way would he do this again, not twice..."

The report loaded, and there it was again:

2e. Organizing Physical Space- Ineffective.

Eric scrolled down.

> **2e. Organizing Physical Space- Ineffective**
> Despite past warnings, teacher remained seated in front of students for the duration of the period.
>
> Teacher instruction would have been more effective if accompanied by circulation around the room to assist students.
>
> Additionally, students were seated in a horseshoe instead of the recommended groups we as a district believe foster student growth and cooperative learning.

It was essentially copied and pasted from the first rating.

Eric shoved his chair back and stood, pacing the room, raging in his head. How could Kirk do this? It was so unfair! Was it too late to challenge the observations? The tenure decision? Surely, any reasonable person would understand his foot was in a cast! *W*

Why hadn't he read this back then? Insisted on a debrief?! *Anything.*

He needed to do something. His whole career, everything he'd worked for, hinged on this tenure decision. It was job security. It was a chance to breathe next year, to spend less time in this building and more living his own life.

It was *nothing*, apparently, because it wasn't going to happen.

Eric strode to the little white phone affixed to his classroom wall and punched in Kirk's extension. It rang and rang while he deliberated his next words. He probably shouldn't shout the guy down, but he wanted to let Kirk know exactly what he thought of him and his fucking *observations.*

The asshole hadn't been in a classroom in over a decade, anyway... The nerve he had even evaluating teachers. He wasn't even the official principal yet, just the interim, still as *probationary* as Eric himself. The more Eric thought about it, the angrier he became. That silent rage, the most dangerous kind, bubbled within him, getting closer to the surface with each unanswered ring.

Finally, he gave up. He placed the phone down too softly, an excess of control stemming from a growing awareness of his anger. Eric took a deep breath and imagined boxing up his rage, storing it in a little container deep in his chest, and buttoning it up. The students would be back soon, and it wasn't for them.

The day was still young. Eric would finish coaching at 4 pm and could find Kirk in his office afterward. The principal was well-known for his tendency to arrive late and leave after most of the building cleared out. Must be nice, Eric thought bitterly, bound as he was to the abnormally early mornings of a public school teacher.

He would finish teaching, coaching, lesson planning, and grading, as he always did, early in the evening. Then Eric would find Kirk in his office, and when he did, he would open up that little box of outrage inside of him and unleash it on the one who deserved it most.

Principal-fucking-Kirk.

RAMONA GIOVANNI

March 30

10:25 AM

Tap, tap, tap.

Ramona curled her toes at the sound. After listening to Will's pen all year, she'd just about had enough. The page before her remained blank, though she knew exactly how to solve the first problem. She lowered her pencil to the paper, doodling a sharp angle above the complicated-looking equation.

A few desks ahead, a soda bottle lay on its side, the dark liquid puddling under Bo's seat, inches from his heavy boots. He remained hunched over his paper in an uncharacteristic display of concentration. Didn't he notice the spill? She couldn't help but judge her classmates in these moments, oblivious as they were. Although, if she were honest, she sometimes felt their parents were the ones she was really judging.

Ramona heard her mother's voice in her head: Ramona Giovanni, you pick that bottle up right now! Who do you expect to clean up after you? I must've forgotten we have hired help! Or, worse, Uncle Donny's face if he saw her do such a thing.

She wondered if anyone ever chastised Bo like that in his house. Maybe he took more care there than he did here. Again, she pictured her uncle's expression, this time with a stab of annoyance at her classmate. It really wasn't that difficult to clean up after yourself.

Tap, tap, tap.

She forced herself to ignore Will, concentrating instead on the folded paper that had just traveled through her classmates from a seat in the front of the room. It landed lightly on her desk and she picked it up, opening it as quietly as possible. Like Bo, most of the class was absorbed in their practice exams, their last opportunity before the actual semester midterm next week.

A little smiley face was drawn hastily beside three words:

Check your phone.

She crumpled the note and pushed it beneath her papers. Ahead of her, Grace flashed a small smile, tucking a blue-streaked blonde curl behind her ear. Ramona sighed and pulled her phone from her pocket just far enough to see her messages.

She didn't want to get into trouble for using her phone in

class. Not after being suspended over morning lateness last month - Her first and only disciplinary action in 13 years of school. She still felt sick over it.

A message from Grace topped her notification panel.

> **Grace:** Cafe Caprese after school?
> **Ramona**: Can't. Have to pick up the brothers.

Grace's reply was instant.

> **Grace:** After?
> **Ramona:** Internship.
> **Grace:** Still doing that? We are basically graduated.
> **Ramona:** It's only March. Still doing it. Maybe tomorrow?
> **Grace:** Yep. Let me know if you skip the internship.

Ramona loved Grace. She was one of her oldest friends. But she just didn't get it sometimes. Grace was going to college because she was *always* going to go to college. Her parents had been preparing her for freshman year before Ramona's mom even enrolled her in kindergarten.

They may have come through the same school in the same town, but Ramona's world was a stark contrast to the one in which Grace lived. She fought and scrounged for every opportunity, every extracurricular, every A that brought her closer to her place as salutatorian. Ramona missed the top spot by inches to someone who didn't have two third-grade brothers to care for while their mother was out making a decent living.

As Ramona closed her messages, another notification caught her eye. She tapped it, and a new email blossomed on the screen. Her heart jumped into her throat as she read the subject line: *Admissions Reconsideration*.

From: smasen@yale.edu
Subject: Admissions Reconsideration

Dear Ms. Giovanni,

Upon receiving notice of your recent suspension from Principal Kirk, we've been forced to reconsider our offerings to you for the upcoming school year. As you know, the Excellence Scholarship is awarded only to incoming freshmen with clean disciplinary records and impeccable transcripts. In light of your suspension, you are no longer eligible for this award.

We also regret to inform you that our Admissions team will review your credentials over the coming week. As stated in the admissions notice you received upon your initial acceptance, we are within our rights to reconsider any applicants with new disciplinary action against them. We will inform you of our decision by the end of next week.

Sincerely,
Sarah Masen
Director of Admissions
Yale University

Ramona shoved her phone back into her pocket as if it had stung her. Sweat broke on her brow, and her stomach lurched. She thought she might be sick. She'd worked so hard for her admission to Yale. And without the scholarship, she didn't see how she'd even afford to go.

Tap, tap, tap.

Ramona whipped around, eyes flashing.

"Cut it out with your stupid pen, Will!"

Heads turned.

"Geez. Sorry, Ramona," Will said, affronted. "I didn't realize it was bothering you so much."

"Well, it is," she snapped. "Cut it out!"

"Fine!"

Ramona spun back in her seat and withdrew her phone again, still hiding it beneath her desk. A message from Grace appeared as she unlocked it.

Grace: All okay?
Ramona: No. Bathroom?

A few minutes later, Ramona sat on the scuffed floor,

knees drawn to her chest. She looked up as Grace emerged through the ugly speckled tile, the door closing loudly behind her. Wordlessly, she handed Grace her phone, still open to the email from Yale.

Grace's eyes widened as she read it.

"Holy shit, Ramona." Grace handed back the phone and sank to the ground beside her. "I'm so sorry."

"I don't know what to do..."

Grace put an arm around her. The tears burning behind Ramona's eyes inched to fall at Grace's touch. She sometimes resented her old friends for the vulnerability they invoked in her with their kindness. She needed to be strong now, not crying on the bathroom floor.

"What do I do?"

"I don't know. Can you speak with Kirk? It sounds like he emailed them or something. The nerve of that fucking guy, after all the work you've done for him..."

Ramona didn't want to think about that now. Didn't want to remember the hours she'd spent in the admin office, building the tutoring program, turning a pipe dream into reality for Cove Harbor High. A tear slipped out, meandering its way down her cheek.

"Oh, Ramona –" Grace wiped it away with her thumb. "We're going to figure this out. Can't you explain yourself? And explain why you were late? It's not like you did anything that bad! Kids are late *constantly*, and you're the first I've ever heard suspended over it."

"You think I can just explain?"

"It couldn't hurt! Let's just write them an email about your brothers and how you need to take them to school. It's not like you're sleeping in or cutting out in the mornings or something!"

"Yeah... Okay." Grace was right, Ramona realized. Maybe she could explain the situation to the Yale Admissions team. Maybe she could even explain it to Principal Kirk and have him reach out on her behalf. A glimmer of hope sparked in her chest.

"Let's get back to class to grab our stuff before the bell. What are you doing next period?"

"Going to physics..."

"I'm skipping out. I want a coffee, and I just have art, anyway. You'll come?"

"No way! I'm not risking any more trouble."

"I was kidding. Have you ever skipped a class in your life?"

A small giggle escaped Ramona as Grace pulled her to her feet.

"I'll work on the email. And I'll talk to Kirk tonight after my internship. He's always the last one in the building. Even if I finish late, he'll be there." Ramona could picture him at his desk, the only one left in a darkening office.

"Good."

Ramona watched her friend leave the bathroom, twisted curls cascading down her back. She leaned over the sink and shivered slightly as cool water splashed over her face. She met her own eyes in the mirror, red-rimmed and a little swollen.

"You can fix this," she told her reflection. "You can make Principal Kirk listen. It's not over until it's over."

GLORIA JENKINS

March 30
11:36 AM

"Thanks," Gloria replied, accepting her hazelnut coffee from the barista. Café Caprese was a one-stop shop for all types of market goods and Italian takeout, but nothing ever quite overpowered the smell of their delicious coffee. She especially enjoyed it on a day like this one, with rain pounding heavily outside and an early spring wind nipping as she passed.

Gloria selected a wide wooden table crammed between a drink cooler and a stainless steel baker's rack of goods. She dropped her briefcase on one of the oversized chairs and collapsed into the other, cracking open her round container of pasta salad. One hand fished in her bag while she eyed three familiar faces in line for coffee.

The taller of the two girls was rolling her eyes at something the other had said, her blue-streaked blonde curls halfway down her back. Grace was her name, and Gloria was willing to bet she was supposed to be in class right now. Gloria pulled her computer from her bag and placed it on the table, opening the screen as she watched the students.

Beside Grace, another senior leaned on the glass display case, his arm around the shorter brunette. Gloria knew their names too, as she did all the seniors and probably every student in Cove Harbor High. Small towns, small schools. And Will and Heather were both extroverted enough to be known around the halls.

Gloria considered reporting them, as a quick search of the school's database confirmed that only Heather had a free period. But then again, she thought, it was spring of their senior year, and what would be the point? She decided against it as she sipped her coffee.

Still, she couldn't stop the nagging voice in her head as she closed the school database. This is why you're still an AP, never a principal. Won't even report three class cutters standing right in front of you.

Gloria silenced the thought, one of the many persistent doubts that had become all too frequent since losing the top job to Kirk last year. She still thought she was the better choice, knew beyond a shadow of a doubt that she was more qualified than Alex Kirk. The snub still stung when she dwelled on it too long.

The students took seats at the next table, too involved in their conversation to notice their AP sitting just feet away, debating whether to report them for skipping school. Heather buttered a bagel, one knee tucked beneath her, while Will dove into a pile of cheese fries.

"What's with Ramona?" Will asked, rolling his eyes, "Since when does she have a problem with me?"

"She doesn't," Grace replied, reaching over and pulling a french fry from his tin container, "She's fine."

"Yeah, right. She nearly took my head off for tapping my pen in Calc..." Will swatted Grace's hand away, upending the ketchup bottle onto the formerly clean tabletop. He righted the bottle, leaving a red smear on the wooden surface.

"She's just..." Grace hesitated, looking around, "She's having a rough day. That's all."

"Oooh," Heather leaned in, "I smell tea. Spill, Grace."

"Well, keep it to yourself, alright. I mean, she'd probably tell you anyway if she were here, so it doesn't matter, but still..."

Will and Heather hung on her words, and even Gloria couldn't help but listen a little more closely. She'd always liked Ramona Giovanni.

"You know how Kirk suspended her for being late? Yale pulled her scholarship. And they might even withdraw her acceptance." Grace's eyes seemed double their size, magnified by concern.

Heather gasped at her words. "No!"

"That bites," Will replied. "Can she fight it? That girl deserves to go to Yale..." He laughed a little. "More than the rest of us, probably, anyway."

"She's going to try. I mean, if I were her, I'd absolutely kill Principal Kirk! That guy has some nerve to report her suspension to Yale after everything she's done for him. It totally pisses me off just thinking about it."

"What do you mean?" Heather looked confused. "Like her internship?"

"Well, yeah, but it's what she *did* in her internship. Remember that tutoring program Kirk was so loud about last year when he was pushing for the principal promotion?"

"The one with the college kids?"

"Yes –" Grace lowered her voice and Gloria strained hard to hear her. "Well, did you know Ramona came up with that? She did basically everything... created the plan, found the college students, and convinced them to join. She even set up the entire website and online platform for the actual tutoring to happen. I'm pretty sure Kirk couldn't run it without her even if he tried."

"No! That sleazy..."

The rest of Heather's sentence was drowned out by Gloria's own thoughts.

She remembered the meeting where Kirk presented the tutoring program that connected local college students with struggling kids at Cove Harbor High. Throughout his lengthy discussion of the Shooting Stars sessions, the participants' ever-improving performance, and the ingenuity of the online platform, Gloria was sure he'd never mentioned Ramona – nor anyone else for that matter.

If Kirk hadn't created that program himself, he had no business taking credit for it. Unless Grace was mistaken. Surely, Kirk couldn't get away with lying so significantly to the board. It would have been an unforgivably underhanded trick.

In fact, hadn't he joked about how difficult it had been to put it all together? Made more than one self-deprecating comment about teaching himself to build an online platform from scratch? Was it possible he was lying the entire time?

Gloria could hardly wrap her mind around it.

Returning to her computer, she opened the shared administrator drive, home to all the board meeting slides and presentations. Kirk's deck about the Shooting Stars program must be saved amongst the crowded files. She opened last year's folder and clicked the October meetings. Nothing. Next, she tried November. Still nothing. Grace groaned in frustration. It had to be here somewhere.

Bingo! December. The final board meeting of the calendar year.

She opened the notes, and there it was, a presentation titled 'Shooting Stars Tutoring Program.' She clicked through slide after slide: introductory info, statistics showing student improvement, screenshots of the online platform. Nowhere was there any mention of Ramona or other student helpers. It was official. Either Kirk lied in this meeting, or Grace was wrong about it now.

And if Kirk lied, he as good as stole the principal's job from her.

Shooting Stars was by far the most significant factor in why he was selected over her for the top spot. Why *he* was given this probationary year to prove he could run the school before they officially appointed him as Cove Harbor High's new principal.

It should've been her.

The easiest thing to do would be to confront Kirk, though Gloria knew it would be a highly unpleasant conversation. The man was beyond defensive and quicker to temper than anyone she'd ever worked with before. There'd be fireworks, and she'd need to be ready for them.

The sudden scraping of chairs startled Gloria back to Café Caprese. Grace, Will, and Heather rose from their chairs, halfheartedly collecting their trash to toss in the can on their way out the door. Gloria opened her mouth, ready to call Grace to her table, question her about Ramona's role in the program.

Then, as she watched Grace flip up her hood, Gloria sat back in her chair. Something didn't feel right about interrogating Grace, especially away from school grounds. She would do a little digging of her own this afternoon and confront Kirk this evening. She didn't need to involve a student.

Gloria knew how to access Kirk's files and didn't think confirming the truth of Grace's claims would be difficult. All she needed to do was wait for his assistant to leave. Vanessa was too loyal to Kirk for her own good, and Gloria didn't want her around for the conversation.

Gloria watched the students leave the Café, a glob of ketchup still smeared on the table where they'd sat. She closed her computer. It was time to head back to her office and find out if Principal Kirk really was as much of an asshole as she'd always suspected.

And if he was... Well, this year was only probationary for him, wasn't it?

A smile slowly stretched across her face. Things were looking up.

JORDAN WHITE

March 30
5:20 PM

"Where are you going?"

Crap.

"Just heading home for the evening!" Jordan forced an upbeat tone. "It's after five!" He waved his umbrella, grinning sheepishly at Principal Kirk's hard stare.

"Jordan. My email?"

He'd hoped to sneak out before Kirk saw him. Jordan had forgotten to resolve Kirk's ridiculous email trouble of the day, but it was already after five and long past time to go. But, on the other hand, he really didn't want to argue with his hot-headed boss.

"Right, yes. I'll get to it now," Jordan grumbled, turning on his heel. What would it be this time, another password reset? Maybe a computer restart? Unbelievable that this inept man was the principal.

"I'll be back in twenty. Just need to collect a few things downstairs."

"Sure," Jordan replied, heading for Kirk's office. The door was propped open, the custodian's cart parked outside. Jordan knocked twice before entering, but the room was empty.

He sat behind the mahogany desk, the only one in the building not constructed of the simple laminate-covered particle board so familiar to high schools everywhere. Dropping his umbrella to the floor, he wiped absently at a condensation ring near the keyboard, but a ghost remained, staining the dark wood. A moment later, Jordan clicked into Kirk's email, ready to wrap this up and head home as soon as possible.

Aha. Kirk was logged in, but the inbox wouldn't refresh. A little message in the corner told him it hadn't synced since yesterday. Jordan sighed, running through the usual quick fixes. It didn't take long to find the problem.

The man's email application was set to "work offline." Jordan couldn't make this stuff up. How had the technologically defunct principal even managed to do that? He cracked a small smile as he toggled off the setting, grateful it hadn't been anything more complicated.

Jordan readied himself to leave, his mind on the Chinese food he planned to pick up on his way home. Before he stood, however, a flood of emails came pinging into Kirk's inbox.

Jordan wasn't a particularly nosy person, and he didn't make a habit of snooping, but one subject line gave him pause. It was a message from Kirk's assistant, Vanessa. Before Jordan knew what he was doing, he'd clicked it.

From: vbonilla@coveharborschools.org
Subject: RE: next year xxxrg

Glad to hear you took care of it. Do I want the details?
-Vanessa

Jordan scrolled down to start the thread from the beginning. The first message was sent from Vanessa to Principal Kirk nearly a month ago.

From: vbonilla@coveharborschools.org
Subject: next year xxxrg

Have you figured out what to do about Shooting Stars next year?

We need that program to work if you want to stay principal and I want to stay principal's assistant. I'm enjoying the upgraded office space. :)

-Vanessa

--

From: akirk@coveharborschools.org
Subject: RE: next year xxxrg

Ramona should be back in our office next year. I'll be creating a new admin assistant position for her.
-Kirk

--

From: vbonilla@coveharborschools.org
Subject: RE: next year xxxrg

Why would she take it? I thought she was going to Yale...
-Vanessa

--

From: akirk@coveharborschools.org
Subject: RE: next year xxxrg

Don't worry. I don't think she's going to Yale anymore ;)
- Kirk

Jordan wished he hadn't read it. What did that mean, she wasn't going to Yale anymore? Jordan didn't know every student in the building, but he knew Ramona. She was one of the few without a reliable computer at home, and she spent many after-school hours in the computer lab attached to his IT office.

Jordan jumped as footsteps approached. He tapped the keyboard, plunging the screen into darkness.

The custodian's face appeared in the doorway.

"Oh, it's only you. Hey, Gordon."

"How are ya, Mr. White?"

"Can't complain."

"Same, same."

Jordan woke the computer screen and closed the email thread. A few clicks later, the message was again marked unread, waiting for Principal Kirk to find it himself. Jordan picked up his umbrella and gave Gordon a quick wave, hurrying past AP Jenkins' still-lit office and into the hallway.

He pondered the email thread as he traversed the empty school. Had Principal Kirk been insinuating to Vanessa that he knew how to stop Ramona from attending Yale? Or, perhaps, that he already had? He remembered Vanessa's email. What did this have to do with the Shooting Stars program?

Jordan mulled it over as he trotted down the staircase, unease growing with each step. If Principal Kirk did anything to sabotage one of the school's most hard-working students from attending the school of her dreams, he should be fired. Hell, he should be arrested.

Jordan saw Ramona in his mind's eye, surrounded by textbooks, typing away on the school's dated computers. She hardly ever noticed the students clowning around her, fighting for top scores on games he never seemed to be able to block, playing jokes on one another with the text-to-speech function. Ramona worked through it all, unwaveringly focused on her assignments.

And as he pictured her at the computer, Jordan felt something hot and harsh creeping through him. He'd never felt quite as connected to the students as other adults in the building. After all, he was just the IT guy. But Ramona was something special. A different breed, working diligently to raise herself up in the world. Just like he had so many years ago.

Jordan's anger mounted, threatening to boil over as he froze, one hand on the door to the parking lot. Suddenly, he changed course, heading back to the Main Office. He needed to find out what the hell was going on here.

And if Principal Kirk did anything to mess up that girl's future, well, he'd sure as shit have something to say about it.

PRINCIPAL KIRK CLOBBERED

March 30
4:45 PM

A knock sounded on Principal Kirk's door as he placed his iced coffee beside his keyboard.

"Yes?"

"Mr. Haywood is here to see you."

"Send him in, Vanessa."

A moment later, Eric Haywood entered the well-decorated room, lingering awkwardly just inside the doorway.

"Sit, please, Eric," Alex Kirk waved a hand toward the seats in front of his desk.

Eric sat, meeting Kirk's eyes with a cold stare. Kirk sighed. He thought he knew why Eric was here.

"What can I do for you?"

"We need to talk about my tenure application."

"Ah, yes... I heard your probation was extended another year. I'm sorry to hear that."

"Like hell you are. I saw my observation reports. You dinged me for not walking around the room, but my foot was in a *cast*!" Eric hissed the last word.

"I'm sorry, Mr. Haywood, but the teacher evaluation rubric is perfectly clear. I can rate you only on what I see and witness, not what I think or my assumptions about your behavior. You know that by now, don't you?"

"Only what you see? Did you not *see* the cast on my foot?" The color was rising in Eric's face, and he was close to shouting now.

Kirk stood his ground. He couldn't tell Eric he'd needed to mark a few more teachers poorly for an even distribution across the staff. The board would want to see a nice mixture of high and low ratings. Besides, if he marked everyone highly from the get-go, what proof would he have that he helped them grow under his tenure as interim principal?

"Mr. Haywood. If you had a problem with your observation ratings, why didn't you ask to discuss them when we first issued the reports?"

"Because... because... Well, I didn't have a chance. I've been so busy with..." The sentence died in Eric's throat, and Kirk smiled.

"Perhaps next time you should make your personal growth a bit more of a priority."

Eric jumped to his feet, eyes flashing. "What's your problem, Kirk?! Do you not want me to teach here anymore?"

"Please watch your tone, Eric. There is no need to be unprofessional. I've never wanted you to leave our school. I simply want –"

"You know what? I don't care *what* you want. I'm finished with you. If you're principal again next year, I'm out. Out!"

Eric strode across the office and through the door, leaving Kirk alone in the ringing silence. Vanessa appeared a moment later.

"What was that about?"

"Oh..." Kirk felt supremely uncomfortable. He hadn't meant for Eric to quit like that. Hopefully, he'd be back. It wasn't exactly an easy job market for teaching positions in strong suburban schools like this one. "It was nothing, Vanessa. Don't worry about it."

"Ramona Giovanni is here to see you, too. She's waiting outside."

"Send her in."

Vanessa raised her eyebrows at him but complied, backing out of the room with a concerned glance at her boss. Unfazed, Ramona entered, walked quietly to his desk, and took the seat in front of him.

"How can I help, Ramona?"

"Hi, Principal Kirk." Her hand shook slightly where it rested on the mahogany desktop, but her voice was steady. "I just wondered if you would consider contacting Yale on my behalf."

"What about?"

"They revoked my scholarship and are reconsidering my acceptance." Her eyes turned towards the floor. "Because of my suspension."

"I see..."

"I just thought..." Ramona took a deep breath. "I just thought you might be able to tell them my late marks weren't due to laziness, or cutting, or something like that. See, I have to drop my brothers off at elementary school before I come in, so sometimes it makes me late. I swear, that's the only reason."

"I'm sorry, Ramona, but you must accept the consequences of your lateness, and your suspension was one of those consequences. There really isn't anything I can do for you."

"Please – I worked so hard to get into Yale, I -"

"Ramona, this is not a matter of working hard. I know what a hard worker you are. In fact, I was going to offer you a position here with me. Next year, after you graduate."

"A... position?"

"Yes, an assistant's position. You would help Vanessa with daily tasks but primarily be responsible for running the Shooting Stars program."

Ramona remained silent, her eyes searching for meaning in his gaze.

"You want me to work here next year? To run the tutoring program?"

"Yes." Kirk smiled, "What do you think?"

Something shifted in Ramona's expression. Was it anger?

Sadness? Resignation? Kirk hoped for the last one. He needed her to accept his offer.

"I think..." Ramona's voice hardened. "I think I need time to consider it." She rose mechanically from the chair and walked to his door, slowly lifting one foot in front of the other as if moving through grimy sludge.

Kirk leapt from his chair and followed her out, grabbing his iced coffee off the desk as he went.

"Ramona!" He called after her.

"Yes?" Ramona turned to face him, those big brown eyes meeting his. For the smallest second, he felt a stab of guilt. Then it passed.

"Let me know what you decide about the assistant position."

Ramona left the Main Office, exchanging a wave and a sad smile with the custodian as he entered. Gordon treated Kirk to a mean glare as he pushed his cart past him, preparing to clean the Main Office. What was the janitor's problem? But before Principal Kirk had time to dwell on the unexpected hostility, he spotted Jordan White.

"Where are you going?"

"Just heading home for the evening!" Jordan's voice was falsely high. "It's after five!" Kirk glared at him. He didn't really care what time it was, as he'd been unable to receive email all day and Jordan still hadn't fixed it.

"Jordan. My email?"

"Right, yes. I'll get to it now," Jordan grumbled, turning on his heel.

"I'll be back in twenty. Just need to collect a few things downstairs."

"Sure."

Kirk left the Main Office and took the long way down to the cafeteria. A quick sugar rush would keep him focused for the next hour. He placed his coffee on one of the cleanly wiped tables and dawdled by the vending machines, examining each selection before making his choice.

Kirk eagerly tore open the first bag of M&Ms on the walk back to his office, his forgotten coffee abandoned for tomorrow's cafeteria staff to find. He'd hardly entered the Main Office when Gloria Jenkins stepped through her doorway.

"Kirk? We need to talk." He groaned. Jenkins had been rubbing him the wrong way for the better part of a decade, but never so bad as this year. She obviously wanted his job. Too bad.

"What's the matter?"

"I have a few questions for you about the Shooting Stars program."

"Okay..." Kirk glanced towards Vanessa's desk, hoping for an excuse to end his conversation with Jenkins, but it sat empty. She must have gone home while he was downstairs.

"How much involvement has Ramona Giovanni had with the program?"

"Why would you ask me that?" Kirk's nerves rattled. What was she getting at? Could she know? No, it was impossible. Ramona never realized he'd presented the program as his own and she had no reason to mention it to AP Jenkins.

"I heard a rumor today that she basically put the entire thing together herself. And, you know what, Kirk? I've been looking into it. And I think it checks out."

"I don't know what you're talking about, Gloria." *Deny, deny, deny.* She has no proof. It'd be his word against Ramona's. And, well, he was the *principal.* She was just some student.

"I think you do, Kirk, and I think the board will be very interested in this. I seem to recall you telling them all about how *difficult* the setup was for you last year. How absolutely *complicated* it was to build the online platform..."

Kirk's fingernails drew blood as he clenched his fists.

"Are you threatening me, Gloria?" His lips pursed against his teeth. "Are you?!"

"I'm simply asking a few questions." Gloria looked at her watch theatrically. "And, look at the time! See you tomorrow, Kirk. I'll be here bright and early to prepare for my lunch with the board members. I do hope they'll all be able to make it." She flashed him a deep grin before leaving the office.

Despite his best efforts to keep control, Kirk's stomach felt like it had been thrown overboard into a stormy sea. He took a deep breath. Before he released it, however, Jordan came tearing through the Main Office door. Kirk hadn't even realized he was no longer at his computer.

"Great to see you're finished! Did you fix my email?"

"What did you do to Ramona Giovanni?!" Jordan was fired

up, and Kirk stifled his reflex to recoil. Instead he stood taller, throwing back his shoulders and lifting his chin towards the taller man.

"Excuse me?"

"What the hell did you do to stop Ramona from going to Yale?!"

"What? How did you – Wait. Did you read my email?!"

"Answer the question! I don't know what you're playing at, Kirk, but that girl deserved her place at that college, and _"

"DID YOU READ MY EMAIL?!" Kirk was shouting now, sweat rolling down his reddening face. That sneaky bastard read his email! He had no right!

"YES! You know what, I did read it! I'll admit it! It's not half as bad as what you've done if I'm right and you messed up her chances at attending a decent college. How can you live with yourself!?"

"You had no right to read my private email! I'll have your job for this!"

"Or I'll have YOURS," thundered Jordan, standing tall over the principal, umbrella clutched tightly in his hand. "It looks to me like you somehow sabotaged her so she would take some silly position as your ASSISTANT?"

"Get OUT!" Kirk roared, spit flying from his mouth. "Now!"

"I'll go, Kirk, but this is NOT over!" Jordan was fuming. Kirk heard him storming all the way down the hall, crashing his umbrella into the lockers as he went.

The principal fought to catch his breath. Separately, neither Gloria nor Jordan knew enough, but together...

WHACK!

Something hit Principal Kirk in the back of the head. He crumpled to the floor, blood flowing heavily, staining the worn carpet.

WHACK!

One more for good measure.

The custodian stood over Principal Kirk's body, broom clutched in one hand, chest heaving with the effort. Gordon stood in the empty office for a moment, catching his breath. Then, he slowly withdrew his phone from his pocket and typed out a text to his niece.

> **Gordon:** Thanks for picking up your brothers again today. I'll grab dinner for everyone on the way home.

A few seconds later, his phone pinged in response.

> **Ramona:** Thanks, Uncle Donny. See you soon.

A MEMORIAL DAY MURDER

MURDER AT THE PARADE

May 31
9:32 AM

The sun winked off the instruments, glaring into the faces of the surrounding crowd. Nearly every musician's eyes lingered on a tall man in summer whites and a straw fedora, drawn by his authoritative stature and the inviolable focus with which he watched the Cove Harbor Community Band prepare their first notes.

Behind him, a blonde man shifted uncomfortably, looking pointedly away from his wife. Discomfort emanated from where they stood, their view of the band obscured by a freckled redheaded woman looking nearly as unhappy to be there as they did.

They all watched as the band director gulped his bottled water, placing it gingerly at his feet before facing the onlookers. Conversation dwindled under his expectant gaze, silence finally falling, and he spoke.

"Welcome, all!" His voice carried well, hints of a lingering London accent dancing over the breeze. "Thank you for joining us on this beautiful Memorial Day, kicking off the summer in Cove Harbor!"

He cleared his throat as applause rang through the roped-off street, tourists and locals alike cheering for the band, the parade, and the impending season. The parade staff and band members joined the uproar, all except a dark-haired trumpet player glaring at the band director.

The director raised a hand and lowered it again as the noise subsided into silence, broken almost immediately by a loud rasping cough from the back of his throat. A skinny clarinetist fidgeted nervously in his folding chair while the closest onlookers exchanged glances at the harsh and unexpected sound.

"Excuse me," the director muttered, lifting a palm to his reddening face before continuing. "While we are eager to have you here for what is sure to be another wonderful summer, let's not forget the true reason we gather on the final Monday in May."

He paused again, and his subsequent statement seemed ejected forcefully from within, each word more effort than it was worth.

"We would like to invite everyone... to join us on the Wharf after our final piece for a... short service in memory of those who have... fought and died for our country."

A small clatter followed his words, drawing eyes to the

back of the band, where a red-eyed and disheveled woman hurried to pick up her fallen xylophone mallet. The band director didn't seem to notice, his breathing turning rapid and shallow as he rotated to face the band.

He raised his left hand and then his baton, ready to start the music. The percussionists grasped their sticks, and the winds inhaled for their first notes. Everything was still as the crowd waited.

But before he could bring the baton down for the first cue, the band director stumbled forward, falling into the flutists with a resounding crash. A scream erupted from the piccolo player as she jumped to her feet, pointing at her unmoving conductor.

An EMT rushed forward from the parade staff, pushing spectators aside and flinging herself to the ground beside the band director, fingers searching desperately for a pulse.

"He's dead!" she cried, and all who could hear her shook, gasped, and wailed in horror. "Frankie Fenton is dead!"

Amid the chaos, one pair of satisfied eyes looked on without fear, lingering just a moment too long on the bottle of water beside the lifeless body.

PHIL MARTIN

May 28
10:24 AM

"I just don't know what to do with him, Ken."

"It's not up to us. The boy will do what he will, and we must accept it."

"Phil is not a boy anymore! He's 23! He's a man, although you wouldn't know it, the way he wastes away."

"He's just doing his own thing. It could be worse...He's making money, pursuing his clarinet..."

"His clarinet? Hardly. Aside from a few failed applications, what pursuits are you referring to? The entire endeavor has failed, and the worst part is that he doesn't seem to care that he's throwing his life away. He's just sitting around, not even trying to pursue a better life!"

"Well, he's playing in the Community Band, Dory, it's not like he's just moping around the house crying all day. He's got a decent job at Reels, and - "

"Busing tables, playing in a silly little community band, that's not enough! What is he thinking? Phil is no dummy. He could've gone into the family trade with his chemistry marks. He could've done so much more! Gavin doesn't have these ridiculous notions, he's - "

The mention of his *perfect* brother was the final straw for the young man lingering just outside the doorway. College might have been the right choice for his mother and brother, but that didn't make it best for him, too. She would never understand how difficult it was for him, Phil thought. How hard he worked to just barely match what came to others so easily in the classroom.

Phil stomped his feet in a few false steps, letting them echo through the tiled kitchen. He waited a moment before following the sound to his parents glaring at one another over the kitchen island. He swallowed his frustration, feeling it collect in the back of his throat.

"I'm heading into town," Phil said, not meeting his anyone's eyes. "I need to drop off the food bank donations before my shift."

"Here - " Dory thrust a paper bag into his hands. "Bring this to the store, will you? Leave it in the back, by the coffee machine. It's K-cup refills to keep us stocked until the order comes in on Tuesday."

"Sure." Phil took the bag, still avoiding her gaze. He didn't want to see disappointment there. No matter how unfair the origin, it stung every time. He never deluded himself that he would grow into the person she'd always wanted him to be, but he hadn't expected to fall quite so short either.

Phil had been naively sure of himself when he decided not to pursue college, to forgo the student loans of a fancy music degree to forge his own path, but every day he became less certain of his choice. Less confident in himself and his ability to be successful.

Nothing was how he'd imagined it would be.

"What's your schedule this weekend, son?"

"Just working," Phil said, feeling a little foolish as he thought of his brother, home from Duke and preparing for his summer internship with a local law firm. A *real* job. "You know. It's Memorial Day and all that."

"Busy weekend ahead, then?" Ken forced a small smile as he pushed his blonde hair out of his eyes. It was thinning, probably, but still as blonde as Phil's own.

"Yeah." Phil knew his dad was just being nice. They hated that he hadn't gone away to school, hadn't done anything substantial with his life. He still lived in his childhood bedroom, and the way things were heading, it didn't look like he'd manage to move out anytime soon. He was just another loser stuck in Cove Harbor.

Dory rolled her eyes and busied herself with something on the counter. She hardly even looked at him anymore. Maybe he deserved her disappointment, he thought. He'd made so many mistakes. After all, Phil was the one who failed to predict that nobody would audition him without a degree on his resume. He learned the hard way that it didn't really matter how good he was at his clarinet. If you wanted to pursue a steady-paying job in classical music, that stupid, ridiculously expensive piece of paper mattered.

He tucked the paper bag into his jacket pocket before taking a few steps toward the door. He hesitated before forcing himself to turn back to face them.

"Are you guys coming to the parade on Monday?"

"We'll be there, Phil." His dad's promise hung there, in opposition to his mother's determined silence.

"There will be a talent scout there from the Big City Orchestra. He'll hear my solo, and maybe I can get an audition with him if he's impressed." Phil couldn't help the hopeful excitement creeping into his voice.

"That's great!" His dad brightened. "This could be a real chance for you! We wouldn't miss it. In fact, maybe we'll talk the guy up a little, tell him what a local star you are."

Phil's half-hearted smile dwindled as his mom scoffed over the counter. His dad glared at her, but Phil didn't. After so many years, he hadn't expected anything else.

"See you later, then," Phil said, dejected. He knew his mom didn't take him seriously after his countless discarded orchestra applications and persistent failure to find any steady gig outside the restaurants. But this was different... He'd never been *heard* before. Sure, on paper he didn't look like much, but if they *heard* him!

This was his chance to make something of himself. Prove them all wrong. Still, a small sliver of doubt needled his enthusiasm as he imagined his mother's disdain, her back turned to him in the kitchen. He didn't need her to remind him that things didn't typically go as he planned. And maybe she was right. Why should this be any different from the other opportunities he'd blown over the years?

The orchestra rep might not even show. After all, Chrissy said he was on vacation, not formally scouting. And she usually knew what she was talking about, right? A benefit of sleeping with Frankie Fenton, he supposed.

"Off to Reels?" The false pompous voice his brother had adopted since starting Duke reached Phil across the driveway. Asshole.

"Yep," Phil replied without turning around. He didn't need to see Gavin's gloating face. He knew he was the one "winning" life, if you will, and Phil was already sick of it. He couldn't wait for the school year to start again, if only to be rid of his brother for a few months.

"Maybe I'll come by for a drink tonight."

"We card."

Gavin just laughed.

They both knew Gavin would flash the ID of an older classmate on his basketball team, walk right in, and Phil wouldn't say a word. That was the thing about really good athletes... They thought they were as untouchable in life as they were on the court.

And they were probably right, Phil reminded himself, a bitter taste on his tongue. Their paths were forged by scholarships and alumni networks, casting them into all kinds of industries they'd hardly heard of before graduation day. Not Phil, though. He forged his own path, however measly and overgrown it may be.

He yanked open the door of his parents' old Toyota and leaned in to pop the trunk. He didn't mind the old humming engine, as it got him from place to place, but driving it just reminded him he couldn't afford his own. Another failure, another disappointment, another joke for his brother to crack with his arrogant friends.

Phil grunted as he hauled this week's massive donation haul into the trunk. More people than you might think relied on the food pantry in Cove Harbor. Their presence was eternally overshadowed by the wealthy tourists and forgotten entirely by the Gavins of the world.

Never forgotten by the Phils, however, with a front-row seat to the struggle in Cove Harbor's restaurants. Collecting excess from Main Street's shopkeepers and dropping it off each Friday before work was a simple tribute to those unseen. Those like him, working harder than anyone else, just to be looked down upon or mocked by those born for something 'better.'

Phil slammed the trunk closed and slid into the driver's seat, slashed upholstery where he'd once caught the pocketknife he carried in high school. It wasn't the only scar from his younger years, but it was the one he noticed most often. A reminder of how little progress he'd made since his teens.

The Bluetooth chirped as his phone rang through the car. "Hello?"

"Good morning, Phil. How are you?"

He hardly noticed the smooth accent anymore but never got used to Frankie's relentless formality. He thought the older man was probably like that because he was British, but he didn't know anyone else from England to compare.

"I'm good, Frankie. What's up?"

"I'm calling to inform you that I've made a seating change for Monday's parade."

Phil concentrated on the gathering traffic ahead of him.

"Phil?"

"Yes? Sorry, Frankie. I'm driving into town, and you know how the traffic is this weekend. Worst drivers on the planet."

"Oh, yes, Phil. I'm familiar." Frankie chuckled. "I just called to tell you that Chrissy will sit first chair on Monday."

"What?" Phil nearly slammed on the brake. "But what about my solo?"

"As first chair, Chrissy will play the solo."

Anger rippled through Phil at his words. Chrissy! Sub-par Chrissy would play *his* solo, the one he'd spent a year perfecting, in front of the talent scout?! This was so unfair.

He'd had so few opportunities over the past few years and couldn't let Frankie take this one away! He was always backing down, always giving up, settling for the short end of the stick.

His mother's voice rang in his ears: *just sitting around, not even trying to pursue a better life*. Not this time! He wouldn't let Frankie blow this chance for him. Then Phil remembered something. How could Frankie even change the seating? He wasn't the band director anymore.

"I thought you retired! What about Eileen?"

"The board saw fit to reinstate me this weekend. Eileen will have her position back when I return to retirement."

"That's bullshit, Frankie."

"Excuse me?"

"You heard me!" Phil was getting heated now, but he didn't care. This wasn't right! "Chrissy isn't half as good as me and nowhere near ready to play that solo!"

"I've been working on it with her, and I think she is ready to perform."

"Of course, you've been *working on it with her.* You think I don't know what that means, Frankie?!"

"That's no way to speak to your director, Phil." Frankie's voice had taken on a haughty tone. "I don't appreciate your rudeness."

"And I don't appreciate you giving away my solo to some woman just because you're sleeping together! You know I'm a better player than her. I'm going to the board! This can't be allowed!"

"You are free to file an appeal when the board reconvenes next month. However, you will likely be filing it against Eileen, as I do not know how long I will remain as band director."

"So, you're just coming out of retirement for a month?! Why would you - " And then Phil realized. Of course. The Big City talent scout. His voice trailed off.

"Phil, please control yourself."

"Is this about the Big City Orchestra talent scout? What, do you want them to scout you? Or is it for Chrissy? I wasn't under the impression you cared that much about her, honestly, the way you traipse around town..."

"That's enough, Phil. I won't have you - "

Phil lost track of his words as a horn blared and he swerved to avoid an out-of-state driver running a stop sign.

"Whatever, Frankie. See you Monday."

Phil hung up and sped as best he could into the village. He avoided most of the traffic jams, pulling behind Main St and into the Cove Harbor Pharmacy's private driveway.

He trotted up the back steps, still fuming from his conversation with Frankie. This was his opportunity to change his fortune, to show his mother and himself that he wasn't crazy for pursuing his music. For chasing his dream. And he was about to lose it all because the goddamned second chair was sleeping with the conductor.

Phil dropped the paper bag beside the coffee machine, situated under a window into the pharmacy storeroom. His eyes trailed over the endless rows of pill bottles and liquids in the locked space. The key felt like a talisman on his ring, burning a hole through his back pocket.

He thought of Frankie, his smug face, pompous and proud in shameless pursuit of women and whatever else around town. That untouchable aura, so similar to Gavin's. No regard for Phil or anyone else, just doing whatever he desired, taking whatever he wanted. Getting away with treating people like crap, over and over again, and there was nothing anyone could do about it.

His eyes drifted again over the vials and containers in the storeroom.

They were right there. They were so close... And he knew exactly what each one did. What each one *could* do. Chemistry wasn't just his best subject, it was his only subject. This knowledge was in his blood, born of a childhood in these aisles and an often unhealthy interest in the way elements collided.

And with that, a more sinister thought crossed his mind.

Maybe there *was* something he could do about Frankie.

Phil *did* have some power, more than he'd ever understood before, and certainly more than Frankie Fenton could have anticipated. He could feel it, warm like the glow of an early summer sun slowly dawning over the bay.

It would be so easy.

A choice descended from above, resting upon his shoulders.

Phil sighed.

He could do it, you know.

But, then again, *could* he?

CONNOR HARRIS

May 29
11:00 PM

The pounding bass drowned the noise of the packed bar. Connor reigned above the mayhem, taking orders and making drinks, sending them every which way like a well-oiled machine. Nikki's tip-mongering laugh sang over his shoulder as she danced her way around the other half of the bar.

The familiarity of the off-season crowd had vanished overnight, giving way to a plethora of high heels and straw hats flooding in from the streets. Connor hardly bothered getting to know the Memorial Day weekend patrons and this year would be no different. Those who stayed the summer might become regulars, but the others would fade into the forgotten abyss of Cove Harbor tourists.

They were all the same, anyway, Connor thought, popping the top off a liquor bottle.

He'd been at it all day, with no end in sight. Not until September, anyway. Connor didn't hate the tourists. Sure, the traffic was annoying, and some of them were more obnoxious than he'd like, but they made life interesting. New blood and all that. Besides, where else would he make tips like these?

Connor smiled at a pretty blonde eying him from Nikki's end of the bar. She returned the grin hopefully, but he turned back to those directly in front of him. He had his own line, and was busy enough without serving Nikki's patrons as well as his own.

Over the back of the crowd, Connor spotted one of their younger employees directing a tall man with a television camera to the glass-paned patio door. Still gesturing, Phil looked back at Connor, raising his eyebrows at the film crew. Connor chuckled appreciatively. This would be the second summer in a row they opened the season on a reality TV series. He wondered which show it was this time.

Phil ushered the group onto the patio, presumably to film their subjects where there was a little more room to breathe. Taylor walked in as they exited, her red hair and freckles setting her apart from the conventional, boring-looking women surrounding her. She waved enthusiastically, and he waved back, knowing it would be some time before she worked her way through the mass of partiers. They'd be lucky if she made it to him by midnight.

"Gin and tonic, please, Connor!"

Frankie's recognizable accent carried over the heads of

men in linen blazers waiting to order another round of cocktails. Connor's band director was a regular, popping in nearly every night. In fact, Connor thought he was likelier to see him chatting up women at Reels than at band practice.

"On it, my man," Connor replied, pulling Frankie's usual from a high shelf behind the bar.

"Will I see you at the parade on Monday?"

"Absolutely! Got the trumpet all warmed up."

Connor swooped a leather booklet from the bar as he handed Frankie his drink. As he pulled out the signed receipt and tip money, his phone lit up, blaring from its place beside the cash drawer. He shook his hair out of his eyes and unlocked the screen.

Jackie: Working?

The message was from Jackie. He fired off a simple *Yep* in response, but it beeped again before he dropped it back on the counter.

Jackie: Will I see you tonight?

Connor looked around, finding Taylor at a high-top table with her friends.

Connor: Maybe not. Crazy night. Otherwise, tomorrow.

Jackie replied with a quick thumbs up. He hoped she understood.

Connor had planned to break it off with Taylor weeks ago, but it was just too complicated, too likely to explode in a fight he didn't want to have. He never intended to get serious with Taylor, but here they were, technically undefined yet implied in that way people become after so many years of finding their way back to one another at the end of the night.

But now there was Jackie, so refreshingly new and enticingly different. She hadn't known Connor since he was an awkward middle schooler. She didn't care that he was a bartender, or that he stayed out late and preferred to sleep away his mornings. Jackie definitely didn't expect anything more from him. It was all the fun, without any pressure. She was everything he wanted.

Taylor, unfortunately, wanted so much more.

The next few hours passed in a blur of music, drinks, and broken conversation with an occasional old friend or other locals braving the crowds. He tossed back a few shots as he served familiar faces, and one in the kitchen just for fun. He wasn't drunk, but he couldn't confidently call himself sober, either.

Reels slowly emptied as the night dwindled into closing time. Not because people were heading home, but because Kelly's was open next door until four. Finally, the guests thinned out, and Connor took the opportunity to wipe down a few splashes of beer along the bar.

The rag slid over the smooth surface, it's swish audible amidst the quickly emptying stools. Across the room, Taylor and Frankie drank together near the patio. Connor paused, towel held aloft, as Frankie leaned into Taylor, whispering in her ear. He was too far away to hear their conversation, but whatever Frankie said made Taylor step away abruptly, a frown darkening her pretty face.

Annoyance crept through Connor as he watched. Was Frankie coming onto her? Didn't he know Taylor was *his* girl? But, then again, Frankie had also seen him with Jackie. Maybe the band director was confused. Hell, maybe Connor was confused. He was planning to break up with Taylor, anyway, wasn't he?

Frankie met Connor's eye, noticing him watching as Taylor pointed towards the bar. A moment passed and Connor knew what was about to happen just before it did. Frankie said something Connor couldn't hear, and Taylor spun on her heel, glaring at him.

Fuck.

Taylor's heels landed heavily on Reels' dirty floor, her arms swinging as she approached. She pushed her way through the final stragglers finishing their drinks and faced him over the bar, hands on her hips.

"Connor! What the fuck is Frankie telling me about you and the girl from the salon?" Direct and to the point. He always liked that about her.

"Taylor, I'm working." His heart raced faster than his

thoughts. He needed time to think. "Can we do this later?"

"No! Are you messing around with Jackie Feng?"

"Well, I only saw her a few times. I was going to tell you - "

"Oh, well if it was *only a few times*, and you were *going to tell me*, I guess it's fine then!" Her sarcasm hit like a physical slap.

"Look, you know we never really defined anything, and - "

"Never defined anything? How many other people have you been hooking up with for the past five years? Can't be Jackie, she would have been a teenager, no?"

"No, actually, I think she's 25..." He regretted the words the moment they left his lips. Taylor glared at him.

"Whatever, Connor, don't do me any favors. And don't call me again."

"Oh, come on, can't we talk about this, Taylor? Don't walk away like that! I want to work on things!" And as he watched her go, he found he really meant it.

Jackie was fun and all, and he hadn't lied to her. He really did plan to end things with Taylor and he *had* enjoyed spending time with Jackie. But there was something he hated about watching Taylor walk away from him like that, of the anger and finality of her disappearing into the night. It was something in the look in her eyes as she left him, and his unanticipated alarm at the idea of her never coming back.

Taylor had always been his girl, even in their old Cove

Harbor High days. He remembered how she looked back then, lounging on the bleachers, all fiery red hair and long legs. What was he thinking, ending things with her? She was more than just some girl he met at the bar. More than Jackie.

He flung down his towel, snatched up his phone, and tapped Taylor's face in his message list.

> **Connor:** Closing in a few, then I'll meet you at Kelly's. Give me a chance to explain.

After a moment, he added, You look beautiful tonight, btw.

He would catch up to her at Kelly's and tell her it was just a stupid fling with Jackie. It hadn't meant anything. Then they could really lock it down, make it official. Connor and Taylor, for real, at last. He could give her that.

"Connor!" Nikki's voice called from the doorway to the kitchen. "Help me with this?"

"Be right there!"

Connor couldn't help but think it never had to happen this way. If not for *goddamn Frankie Fenton*. Why couldn't he just keep his mouth shut? As if there weren't plenty of other available women for him to meet tonight. As if Connor hadn't covered for him a hundred times, had his back with more conquests than he could count.

Even when Frankie slept with the xylophone player, Connor didn't say a word. And Connor heard things at the bar. He knew that woman's mental health was dicey at best, and he was pretty sure Frankie even convinced her to pay off some of his personal loans. Dave from the bank had told Connor the whole shady story one slow, late night last winter.

But, even then, did Connor say anything? Did he sell Frankie down the river? Of course not. Because that's not what bartenders do. That's not what *people* do, especially local people in a town overrun by outsiders. But apparently, Frankie Fenton doesn't care about any of that. He clearly didn't give a damn about anyone but himself.

Connor imagined an angry and upset Taylor over at Kelly's. She was probably telling her friends all about it, laying out what a dick he was. Maybe others would overhear. Maybe some asshole guy would seize the opportunity, take advantage of her desire to get back at him for sleeping with Jackie. The idea made him feel hot and cold all at the same time, anger competing with dread inside him.

He seized his rag again, this time tackling the other end of the bar. His mind swirled as he scrubbed violently at the wood, one solid thought standing out amongst the rest: This was all Frankie Fenton's fault.

Goddamned Frankie Fenton.

BRANDY PHILLIPS

May 30
8:00 AM

Brandy stepped lightly over the uneven sidewalk, carefully lifting her worn sandals over each crack. *Step on a crack, break your back!* She sang the ditty in her head as she walked, remembering classmates chanting the tune as they skipped through the streets of Cove Harbor. Could those happy days really have been forty years ago? It seemed impossible.

She looked up guiltily at the Cove Harbor pharmacy as she passed, echoes of the incessant reminders she'd ignored over the past few weeks replaying in her head. *Pick up your prescription!* said her calendar app. *Don't forget to take your meds!* said her sister. *I'm worried about you!* said her mother.

But she was fine, truly. She'd been fine for a long time now. She knew herself better than anyone else did, and she would know if it was time to take those pills again. Who needed them when you were so happy and in love as she was?

She'd made so much progress.

Besides, the non-prescription strategies were really working wonders lately. Meditating in the gardens, dwindling her trust fund on new plants and everything she needed to care for the most complicated among them. She was doing things that made her happy - Like her Sunday breakfast ritual.

A doctor couldn't prescribe everything, you know.

Brandy tightened her grip on the paper bag in her hand. She couldn't wait to see Frankie's face this morning. They'd finally had his favorite bagel at the shop. They'd been all out of spinach-everythings for the past six weeks, but not today! It would be a good day. She could feel it.

She soon reached Frankie's house, but passed by, heading instead to the nearby deli that stocked his preferred coffee roast. He loved an aromatic blend popular in Europe, and today she ordered one for herself, too. It smelled like heaven.

Brandy balanced the drinks carefully in their tray while she dug through her wallet for enough quarters to pay. She had her credit card, of course, but these pesky coins were always a bother to carry around. It was only a matter of time before they took an accidental spill, and then where would she be? Embarrassed and scrambling, that's where. No, it was better to get rid of them now.

She dropped the small pile loudly on the counter, nudging each one as she counted the change. The white-haired man at the register smiled at her.

"Don't worry about it, Brandy. Bring me a pretty plant next time you come in, and we'll call it square."

"Sure thing."

She stopped counting and pushed the coins towards him.

"How are your parents? Doing well, I hope?"

"They're great! Just finished updating the back wing of the house."

"Ah, yes, I noticed the construction. And your greenhouse? All prepped for the summer season?"

"Absolutely!" Brandy always appreciated Mr. Knull's interest in her gardens, especially the exotic greenhouse she maintained in the far part of their property.

She gathered the coffees and stepped into the sun, the Knull Deli's bell clanging on the door closing behind her. It was sunny and warm, warmer than it had been so far this year. She should've ordered an iced tea, she thought regretfully, imagining the refreshing cold of the sweet drink.

Brandy hopped lightly up Frankie's front porch, pausing momentarily at the top of the steps. A vine crept its way around the post, winding up to the roof to climb the worn shingles. Wide white and pink roses blossomed along it like the crown a beautiful bride might wear on an early summer wedding day. How beautiful, Brandy thought, running her finger along the plant.

Ouch! A spurt of blood appeared as her skin snagged on a thorn. She sucked on her finger, the coffee tray balanced precariously in the crook of her elbow. The metallic taste mixed with the fragrant roses, an ominous combination in the sweet air of late May.

Brandy jumped, nearly toppling their drinks, as the door opened behind her. A tall redhead emerged, a pair of heels in two fingers and her head bent low. She blushed as she saw Brandy, and then hurried to help her, her bare feet padding lightly over the porch planks.

"Here, let me take those!"

"Thank you!" Brandy smiled appreciatively as the girl placed the tray of coffee on a glass table in the corner of the porch. She looked as though she'd been crying. "Are you alright?"

"Yes," she said. "I'm fine."

"Are you sure? You seem upset."

"I just - Well, I just did something I'm not proud of." The woman nodded towards the house. "Or *someone* I'm not proud of, anyway." She managed a weak smile, but Brandy didn't return it.

"Well, I'd better go," the redhead said, "See you around." And she hurried down the steps, still swinging her heels by their ankle straps.

"Brandy?" Frankie's voice called from behind the screen door.

"Hi, Frankie!" Brandy picked up the coffee tray, but Frankie waved her down.

173

"No, no, Brandy, let's sit outside this morning." He took a seat at the table, his flannel robe open against pajama pants and a white t-shirt. "Mm-mm, the smell of coffee in the morning."

She smiled as he inhaled the caffeinated aromas drifting from the cup.

"Who was that?" Brandy's voice squeaked awkwardly.

She opened the paper bag and passed Frankie his spinach-everything bagel. A terrible sense of unease was falling over her like a heavy blanket, smothering her earlier joy, weighing her down.

"Oh, I don't know. Tammy, or Taylor, or something like that."

"I'd think you would know her name." Brandy felt cold at the thought of that freckled redhead spending the night with her Frankie. But then, a better thought: At least Frankie knew *her* name. She tried to concentrate on that.

"Is everything alright, Brandy? You seem upset."

"I'm getting tired of it, Frankie." Panic flashed through her for a moment as she realized Frankie didn't even know why she would be upset about his overnight guest. But then, just as suddenly, it was gone, replaced by a faint irritation and the persisting uneasiness she knew so well.

"Tired of bagels?" His joke only made her feel worse.

"Tired of waiting."

"I see," he said, pausing to pull the wax paper off his bagel. Her own breakfast sat untouched in front of her. They sat in silence a few moments longer before he met her eyes.

"Brandy, may I ask what you think we are doing on Sundays? What you think this is?"

"What do you mean, Frankie?"

"Well, I enjoy our bagels, of course, and I think you are a lovely person and a wonderful xylophone player, but - "

"Thank you, Frankie," Brandy accepted the compliment, smiling through the dread forming in the pit of her stomach. Something terrible was coming. *No*, she told herself. *Everything is okay. Nothing bad is happening*. She held on tight to the notion.

"Brandy, wait - I wasn't finished. I love our Sundays together, but you know... I mean, you do know that this is purely platonic, don't you?"

She struggled to make sense of his words. *Nothing bad is happening.*

"Platonic?"

"Yes - I mean, we are only friends, you see?"

"Friends?"

"Um, yes. Friends."

"Friends... for now, you mean? I know you enjoy meeting women at the bars, and I wouldn't dream of standing in your way, but... it's only temporary, right?"

Nothing bad is happening.

Frankie wasn't smiling anymore.

"Brandy, I'm sorry if I gave you that impression. But I've only ever been interested in friendship with you. I thought I made that perfectly clear at band practice and the first time you brought Sunday breakfast. Don't you remember?"

She wasn't listening.

Nothing bad is happening.

"Brandy?"

"No, Frankie! You and I are meant to be! The xylophone player and the conductor! The perfect love story! Right?! We'll be together when you're finished - "

Frankie rose to his feet, looking uncomfortable. "Brandy, maybe it's best you go. I'm sorry. I thought I'd been clear about this. I thought - "

"You thought I was just another fool you could throw aside! Like that stupid redhead!"

"Brandy!"

She didn't know where her anger came from, she never knew, but the floodgates were breached, flung wide open for the storm.

"How dare you! You cannot make a fool of me!"

She flung her cup at Frankie, who ducked and shifted to avoid it. It crashed into the porch rail and popped open, staining the roses brown with hot coffee, no trace of their earlier sweetness remaining. They smelled only of death now, and funerals.

Shock emanated from Frankie as his eyes moved from her face to the fallen cup and back again. "Brandy!" he said again, and the horror in his voice stopped her short.

Her anger vanished, replaced by a growing melancholy opening like a chasm within her. She longed to fall into it, crawl into bed, and wrap herself in the throes of indifference.

"Why, Frankie?" Tears were starting.

"Why, what?"

"Why not me?" Brandy was spiraling. This was the end.

"I'm sorry, Brandy, it's just - I have a type, you know, and..." his voice trailed off.

She was already descending the steps, wiping away the mascara running down her face. She didn't need him. She couldn't have him. Well, if she couldn't have him, nobody should.

A determined sort of hostility was growing within her, like a hard pit in the center of her chest. It manifested as she walked home, through the house, and into the backyard. All the way past her mother's flower beds, and into the greenhouse where she tended her most obscure plants.

The air inside was clear and aromatic, every life within nestled happily in its perfect place. They waited for Brandy, her nurturing, loving care born of infinite devotion and a delicate touch. Her plants were just like her, she thought, as she visited each one in its bed of soil, singing softly to them. Colorful and unique. Unmistakably beautiful, yet at the same time, far deadlier than they seemed.

EILEEN JOHNSON

May 31
6:35 AM

Eileen pulled into an empty spot behind the white brick building where the Community Band played, relieved the lot was still nearly empty. She didn't know why she was even here. They had some nerve expecting her to show up after ousting her like they did. But she was still part of the band, and she wouldn't miss one of their biggest events of the year.

She pulled open the back door and followed the narrow hallway to the band's practice room. People crowded the red, white, and blue display under the window basking in the sounds and smells of summer drifting from the open panes.

A folding table creaked the massive continental breakfast towering with pastries and baked goods. Eileen glared at two older men beside it, one passing a blueberry muffin to the other.

"Hey!"

She turned to see Jeanie seated behind her, all three pieces of her flute held aloft. Eileen gratefully took the seat next to her friend, stretching out her legs as Jeanie carefully cleaned the silver instrument. She smiled at Eileen as she pushed her fluffy purple wand in and out of the hollows.

"Good morning, Jeanie. How's everything?"

"Can't complain. But I should really be asking *you* that. How are you holding up?"

"Fine. Pissed, but fine."

"I get it. I know what this meant to you, leading the band in front of that Big City Orchestra scout."

"Are we even sure he's coming?" Eileen almost wished he wasn't.

"Chrissy seems to think so. Apparently, he rented a place outside the village and posted online that he'd be staying to see the parade today."

"Right." Eileen tried to push back the crushing disappointment. It wasn't an official scouting trip, anyway. He might not even listen to the band.

"So, what happened?" Jeanie lowered her voice. "Did they just call you up and say Frankie wanted the job back? Was there a reason?"

"No clue. You know those old geezers on the board never liked me. They were just waiting to get a man back up there, fit the image in their ancient heads."

Eileen looked up at the two men. They'd left the breakfast

table, but continued chatting away, oblivious to her arrival. She knew only 13% of all conductors in the US were women, and after this experience, she was starting to see why.

For all the pomp and circumstance around inclusion and equality, at the end of the day, decision-makers imagined their musicians directed by a man. And until that changed, she'd have trouble breaking into any prominent orchestra.

Jeanie nodded. "Don't we know it.."

"It was always a long shot, but I really thought this could be something great for me. The Big City Orchestra is making headlines right now with its efforts to embrace gender equality and join the 21st century. I thought, maybe if this guy heard us, saw me up there, I could get an audition..." Her words faded as the image of what could have been drifted away.

"I'm so sorry, Eileen, truly. Want me to whack Frankie with my flute?"

"Yeah," Eileen laughed. "Then they'd have to get me up there to replace him."

"The show must go on!" Jeanie's giggle made her smile. Old friends had a way of eliciting joy, even on the hardest days.

"Eileen!" She looked up as Alan, still chewing the last of that blueberry muffin, beckoned her over. He seemed happy enough to see her, considering he was the one who reinstated Frankie in her position just a week earlier. Eileen rolled her eyes at Jeanie and rose from her seat.

"Yes, Alan?"

"I was hoping you could help us out today."

"Really?" Eileen's face lit up. Surely if anyone could give her the top job back, it was Alan Gladman, chairman of the Community Band board. "You mean...?"

"See those cases of water over there?"

Her excitement died in her throat. "Yes..."

"Would you mind distributing those? Keeping everyone well hydrated? It's a hot day, and a long parade."

"Oh," Eileen glared at him. "Sure."

"Great. A cooler is already waiting for you outside near our concert space."

The Community Band didn't even walk in the stupid parade. They just waited and played at the end. Couldn't everyone get their own waters?

She stalked over to the stacked case, ripping open the one on top and pulling two bottles from the tight plastic. Eileen returned to her seat, thrusting a bottle at Jeanie.

"Here - I am officially your water girl."

"No way," Jeanie replied. "He's got some nerve, he does."

"Tell me about it."

Jeanie tucked her cleaning wand back into her case.

"I'm going to grab a cup of coffee before they run out. Remember last year? Never again." Jeanie laid her flute across her seat and set off for the coffee pot, half full beside a stack of paper cups.

Eileen watched the musicians prepare as she waited for Jeanie to return. The energy seemed off today, but she couldn't put her finger on what was wrong. There was just something unpleasant in the air.

Across the room, Connor clutched his trumpet tightly in one hand, snarling amid his heated conversation with Frankie Fenton. Good, she thought. Give him hell from me, the sneaky bastard. Why did Frankie even give up the band director position if he still wanted it? She hated him for that. And for the hope she'd had, only to be snatched away on his whim.

Eileen's attention turned to Jeanie, now chatting with Chrissy by the coffee station. She should get a cup, too. It would settle her nerves. But first, she'd check the talent scout's social media profile to see if he'd posted from the parade. A fruitless refresh of his page, still open on her phone, told her nothing new had appeared.

Crash!

Eileen looked up in alarm as a young clarinetist collided with Brandy, the xylophone player, hardly three feet away.

"Sorry!" Phil cried, bending low to help Brandy retrieve the items spilled from her purse. Eileen raised her eyebrows as Phil piled various orange pill bottles back into Brandy's denim satchel. Even stranger than the medications, however, was the handful of purple flowers littering the floor. Brandy quickly collected them, pushing them deep into the folds of her purse before hurrying away.

"Thank you, thank you," Brandy called as she went. Her hair was wild around her face, and she looked like she hadn't slept. Poor woman. She seemed like she could use a break from whatever was keeping her up at night.

The next hour passed uneventfully as the musicians finished breakfast and made their way outside to the folding chairs arranged in front of the sparkling marina. She grasped the first case of water in both hands, heaving it outside to the cooler.

She dropped it heavily, then surveyed the scene. It was a beautiful morning for a parade, and for their outdoor concert. The sun glittering over the boats still took Eileen's breath away, even after a lifetime in this little village.

She stood a few steps from the band, pulling up a chair by her cooler of bottled water. Every so often, she pulled one out, cracked it open, and handed it off to a thirsty musician. Her anger grew with each distributed bottle, festering and mutating in a quiet fury. She was a conductor, a *professional*, not an intern, for goodness sake.

Eileen scanned the crowd accumulating in front of the band, expanding with the approaching parade. Onlookers nudged past one another seeking the best spots from which to watch them play. Before long, Eileen spotted the Big City Orchestra scout sauntering over, looking just like he did online.

She couldn't believe it! He was really here! He would listen to them play!

And she was handing out water. Unbelievable.

If only there were some way that bastard Frankie Fenton would retire again, right here, right now. Or at least sit this one out. Maybe she could ask him. He had no real reason, after all, to want to conduct today. He would probably return to retirement soon enough. But, for her... This was truly a once-in-a-lifetime opportunity.

"Frankie!" She jumped from her seat before she could change her mind, heading him off as he walked towards the front of the band. "Frankie, wait!"

"Good morning, Eileen." Just hearing that accent made her burn with anger. He thought he was so smooth, so perfect.

"Hello, Frankie." Eileen stood tall. "I was wondering if you would mind if I led the band this morning. Even if just for one piece. See, there's a talent scout here from the Big City Orchestra, and I would love the opportunity to conduct for him. This could be really important for my career."

He cocked his head at her.

"Your career?"

"Yes, Frankie, my career - It could mean an audition at the Big City Orchestra! I'd *kill* for that."

He studied her for a moment, letting his eyes drift from her thrifted blazer down to the slacks she'd had pressed for today. She shifted uncomfortably under his displeased smirk. And then...

"No, Eileen, I don't think so. I would like to lead the band today. Maybe another time."

Frankie attempted to walk around her, but she stepped in his way.

"There will not be another time, Frankie! This is it. Now or never."

"Well, then, Eileen, I suppose the answer is never. If you'll excuse me."

He left her standing there, fists clenched and seething. What was his problem? She stomped back to the water cooler, trying to control her temper. Eileen's eyes fell on a jumble of Brandy's personal items carelessly discarded on the pavement near the bottled water. Eileen remembered the prescription bottles within and an idea occurred to her. A simple, crazy idea.

What would it really take to put Frankie Fenton to sleep for a few hours? They would need a backup conductor... and here she was. The only question now was whether she had the nerve to do it.

Eileen reached into the cooler, fishing through the ice. She took a deep, resigned breath and withdrew a bottle of water, slowly cracking it open.

FRANKIE, FINISHED

May 31
9:02 AM

Connor stomped through the parking lot, already regretting his decision to come here. How could he face Frankie Fenton? Look him in the eye? Play in his band like nothing happened? After all the years of covering for him in the bar and helping him out. That asshole had some nerve sleeping with Taylor.

It wasn't Frankie's fault. It was YOUR fault. As if you have a leg to stand on after Jackie Feng.

Taylor's angry words echoed in his mind, but he pushed them away, silencing the noise. He'd been with Jackie before he realized how much he needed Taylor.

It wasn't the same as her going home with Frankie. Not even a little bit.

Connor brooded over the situation as he fixed the mouthpiece into his trumpet, just feet from where Frankie stood. His mind hummed with anger, a persistent background noise to every thought and emotion as he glared at his conductor's haughty posture. Connor hated the man's gross cockiness, ever pretentious with that oh-so-superior aura emanating from each thread of his stupidly expensive suit.

Without warning, Frankie turned, meeting his eyes. Frankie's lips twitched, slowly twisting into a smile. Connor pictured them on Taylor's and the anger boiled over, driving him to his feet. He reached Frankie in seconds, trumpet still grasped firmly in his hand like he was ready to smash the man over the head with it.

"What's your problem, Frankie?"

"Excuse me, Connor?"

"You heard me! What's your deal? Telling stories about me to Taylor? Sleeping with her?" Connor was breathing heavily now, just inches from Frankie's no-longer-smiling face.

"I don't know - "

"Don't tell me you don't know what I'm talking about!" Connor could hear himself getting louder, but he didn't care.

"Shh, Connor. You're making a scene."

"Oh, are you worried someone will hear? Chrissy? Brandy? How many other women in this room are you keeping secrets from? None much longer, if I have anything to say about it! You don't want to start this type of shit with the bartender, Frankie, I'd think you'd have learned that over the years!"

Frankie stared at him, stunned silent. A moment passed, and then another. Until -

"Are you quite finished, Mr. Harris?"

"I - "

"I would suggest you get control of yourself. Otherwise, I'll have to ask you to leave." Frankie turned on his shiny leather heel and stalked off, leaving Connor fuming behind him.

Connor collapsed back into his seat and tried to quell the fury still raging in his mind. Frankie walked away, smiling and mingling with the board members before joining Chrissy at the coffee station. That asshole...

Wham!

Connor's mental railing against Frankie was broken by someone slamming into the back of his chair.

"Watch it!" he snapped at the flustered xylophone player, then instantly regretted his tone.

"S-Sorry, accident," Brandy mumbled.

"It's alright," Connor waved his hand, "No big deal."

Brandy kept moving, not bothering to reply as she rushed across the room and into the hallway. She opened the small bathroom door, dropping her bag loudly on the counter. Her hands shook as she rummaged through the clutter inside.

Six orange pill bottles sat amongst the crumpled papers and remnants of her life, all with different labels and varying amounts of tablets inside. Brandy picked them up, one by one, deciding which to take.

She was losing track of things, but not so much as to be unaware she'd taken a few too many since Frankie said those awful things yesterday. She'd needed them. But now she couldn't remember which way was up and she didn't have the nerve to ask for help. Her mother would be so infuriating about the whole thing.

Finally selecting a container, she shook a few tablets into her palm, hardly reacting as one bounced into the sink. Brandy ran the water and watched the little pink disc slide and melt across the tinged porcelain.

She reached inside her satchel, fumbling until her fingers found the purple flowers. It was her favorite plant in the garden. Beautiful, yet deadly. And it gave her simple pleasure to have something so discreetly powerful in the palm of her hand. She took a deep breath, calmed by the belladonna's presence, its leaves smooth against her fingers.

Everything is okay. Nothing bad is happening.

Brandy stared at her reflection in the mirror. Her eyes glowed red and puffy from 24 hours crying over stupid Frankie Fenton. Could she ever stop loving him? She ran her fingers through her tangled hair before admitting defeat. She was hopeless.

Without warning, intense anxiety gripped her, seizing her stomach and manifesting in clenched teeth, biting hard on nothing. It was thick and heavy, yet frantic all at once. Her chest tightened as her breathing got away from her, shallow and fast when she needed it to be slow and deliberate.

She was going to be late! Miss her cue. And where were her mallets? She flung everything into her satchel and rushed from the bathroom, charging back into the band's practice room.

Crash!

She collided with a young blonde man holding his clarinet case. Heads turned as Brandy fell to the ground, sprawling beside her spilled belongings.

"Sorry!" Phil cried, bending low to help Brandy retrieve the items tumbled around her. They'd scattered further than she realized.

"Thank you, thank you," Brandy sputtered as she got to her feet.

Surprise crossed Phil's face as he collected the pill bottles strewn about the floor. He'd helped enough in his parents' pharmacy to know Brandy was a regular, but this seemed like an awful lot. And what were those flowers? They couldn't be nightshade? Could they?

Well, he wasn't one to judge. Not today.

The crushed pills in his own pocket weighed him down with purpose and what was still to come. But... did he have the guts to go through with his plan? Did Frankie really deserve to die for what he'd done? Sure, taking away first chair wasn't that bad on its own. But if there was one thing Phil recognized in this world it was a bully. And Frankie Fenton sure as hell was one.

People like that, sauntering through life, doing whatever

they pleased, taking what they wanted and stepping all over the lives of those deemed beneath them... They deserved every last thing that came their way. Every ounce of misfortune, every inch of pain.

He thought of his mother, how she hated him for not choosing college. He thought of his brother's gloating face as he accepted his full ride to Duke (and life) based solely on traits he managed to be born with. Not like Phil. Measley as his list of successes was, he'd worked long and hard for every last thing he had.

Near the breakfast buffet, Frankie sipped his coffee, leaving it on the table before crossing the room to chat with Chrissy. The sight of them together only fueled Phil's anger. A few minutes later, Frankie returned to the coffee cup, taking another sip before abandoning it again, this time for a visit to the restroom.

Phil touched his pocket where the little baggie rested.

He could do it, you know. He could do it so easily. For every poor shmo out there who Frankie trampled over the years. For everyone like himself, stuck in this little town, looked down on by those who'd gotten out and those who'd managed to succeed here.

He could do it for all of them, for everyone just like himself.

But, then, what would that make him? The internal conflict raged. Could Phil really kill someone? Would that make him just as bad as Frankie? And Gavin? And all the others like them? His intentions undulated like a pendulum as he fit his clarinet together and prepared to join the band outside.

Finally making his decision, Phil turned his back on Frankie's unattended coffee, departing the building to find his seat. He stood to the side, waiting for an opening in the aisle where his folding chair waited for him.

It was better that the little bag of powder was still in his pocket. For the best, really. He wasn't a killer. He was a good guy.

Behind him, he heard Eileen's voice calling to Frankie.

Phil always liked Eileen. She was like him, always looked down on, probably because she wasn't as formidable a conductor as Frankie. Although his mom said it was because she was a woman in a man's field. Phil thought she might be right, though he didn't pretend to know much about gender equality in the world of conductors.

Phil listened as Eileen asked, no begged, really, for Frankie to let her lead a piece. The longing and desperation in her voice was so apparent, so raw, Phil thought for sure Frankie would oblige. But, then...

"No, Eileen, I don't think so. I would like to lead the band today. Maybe another time."

Phil's outrage grew as Frankie so casually ripped Eileen's dreams away, tearing them down like they meant nothing, like *she* was nothing.

This was what Phil was talking about! No regard, no care. Just pure selfishness.

He wrung his hands, fidgeting where he stood. He

should've done it, Phil thought. He hated that he'd hesitated, hated his cowardice and determination to be "good."

Maybe being the "good guy" wasn't as clear as it seemed. Maybe there was a little gray area between that black and white, hovering just within reach.

Before Phil knew what he was doing, he slipped the little baggie up his sleeve the way he'd practiced that morning in the car. He walked over to where Eileen had returned to the cooler, a place as fine as any to let her talent waste away to nothing.

She pulled a water bottle from the icy depths.

"Can I have that, Eileen?"

"Sure," She handed Phil the bottle of water, newly cracked open. "Good luck out there."

"Thanks," he replied, turning his back on the band. Facing the white building, he could see the masts of the boats reflecting in the wide windows, a mirror image of the beautiful marina behind him. He opened the bottle and held it in front of his stomach, raising his other elbow as the powdered contents of the little baggie under his sleeve swirled into the liquid.

Tightening the lid, he shook it lightly as he walked to the front of the band where Frankie stood adjusting his bow tie. He stole only one glance at the bottle as he went, a fraction of a second, barely long enough to confirm it didn't look suspiciously discolored or cloudy. It was good enough.

"Here, Frankie - " Phil offered him the bottle. "Sorry about the other day. I didn't mean to be so rude on the phone."

"Thank you, Phil. I appreciate your apology. I know it can be difficult to stop our emotions running away with us, but I must insist you keep yourself in check in the future."

"Sure thing," Phil replied, discarding the criticism with his lingering shreds of guilt. He turned his back on the conductor, finally taking his seat amongst the other clarinets.

Second chair.

Up ahead, Frankie Fenton looked out over the marina, satisfaction all over his face. Smiling, he took a deep sip of his water bottle and prepared to address the waiting crowd.

A SHOT IN THE CROWD

A SHOT IN THE CROWD

July 26
3:52 PM

An uneasy crowd gathered before the podium, solitary atop the Municipal Building staircase. All left their homes and jobs on this sweltering afternoon for the mayor's impromptu press conference, the first of its kind in many years.

A stocky red-headed man exchanged a nervous glance with a curvy woman as his hand moved inside his jacket. Her eyes stared determinedly beneath her bright purple eye makeup, a captivating contrast to her dark hair. A teen near the far sidewalk glared shamelessly at the tinted windows of a small white car parked a few spaces down.

They all refocused on the podium as Mayor Clark emerged from the Municipal Building and took her place behind it. The usually formidable woman looked tiny, standing alone beneath four stories of red brick baking in the summer sun.

A thud echoed through the street as she tapped the microphone. Silence fell but for the rustling of the Cove Harbor Express reporter's notebook, pages hastily flipping as the mayor prepared to speak.

Someone coughed.

"Welcome, everyone. Thank you for joining me today on such short notice."

A moment of hesitation followed as the mayor glanced up at the building across the street. Surprise fleeted across her face before her expression settled into anxiety and dread for her words to come.

"I called you all here today to tell you something difficult, but important. I - "

Crack!

A shot rang out, followed by two more in quick succession.

Mayor Sue Clark's eyes widened in shock as blood blossomed across her chest. She crumpled, dead before she hit the ground, and chaos erupted around her.

JOHN SCOTT

July 26
9:45 AM

The ticking clock cut the quiet of John's cramped office as he mulled over last month's receipts. His foot wiggled while he ticked away the numbers, making notes in the computer program Danny set up for him last summer. It really did make life easier, he thought, as the flashing blue and white screen calculated his total sales.

He leaned back in his chair and pushed the heels of his hands into his eyes. He breathed deeply, inhaling hot, musty air and watching spots dance in the darkness. John didn't need some fancy computer program to tell him what he already knew. If something didn't change, this would likely be the last season for Scott's Grocery.

A knock rapped on the door.

"Dad?"

"Come on in, Bo," he replied.

"Thought you ought to see this."

Bo tossed a newspaper onto the cluttered desk. It landed on his keyboard with a clatter, joining the other haphazardly strewn paperwork he'd been avoiding all week. The dark headline jumped off the page.

MAYOR LIKELY TO APPROVE BOX STORE TO BREAK GROUND AUGUST 10

He groaned. Tearing his eyes from the paper, John raised a hand to stop his son from leaving.

"Hang on... Why aren't you at summer school?"

"Oh, come on, Dad, I'm basically finished. I don't think a morning here or there will stop Island Community from letting me in next fall." Bo laughed, but John didn't crack a smile.

"Where's your brother?"

"He left before I did. I thought he'd be here by now."

John looked out the window at Danny's empty parking spot.

"Alright. Thanks, Bo."

His son left the office, banging the door shut behind him.

John glared angrily at the newspaper resting on his keyboard. He snatched it from the keys and crumpled the front page, focusing on it just long enough to register Sue Clark's smiling face plastered above the fold.

He didn't need another article about the wonderful things the grocery chain would bring to Cove Harbor. Definitely didn't want to read about their promise of new jobs, or affordable inventory. That place wouldn't bring anything good for the Scotts, that's for sure.

He thought of his sons, giving up their dreams of faraway universities to study here and become the fourth generation to run Scott's Grocery. He thought of himself doing the same so many years ago. Did he regret it? Would his boys? It would be his fault if they did.

A jolt of anger unsettled him. Why was Sue Clark supporting the giant retail complex anyway? He knew her... He voted for her! They went to high school together. Even hooked up once or twice, if he remembered correctly.

She was supposed to protect the local shops, not sell them out.

That's why they elected her. She *knew* Cove Harbor. She would understand the local community, protect them. That had been some lie they'd eaten up. Now in office, Sue would instead be the ruin of this town. Of him, his family, and how many others like him? He still struggled to believe it. Sue was better than this, once.

John threw the crumpled page at the wire mesh basket across the room. It bounced off the rim and skidded across the floor. Typical. He yanked his phone from his pocket, fumbling slightly over the screen as he dialed Danny's number.

Straight to voicemail.

Strange. Bo was always forgetting to charge his cell, but Danny? He was the responsible one. The one who got things done, no matter the cost.

"Hey, Danny, it's Dad. Just checking in to see where you are. Call me when you get this."

He hung up and dialed another number.

"Hello?" Her voice still made him smile, despite the decades spent and the trouble they were in.

"Hey, Becca. Have you heard from Danny?"

"No... He left over an hour ago. He's not at the store?"

"Not yet," John replied. "We were expecting him at nine."

"I'm worried about him, John. He's been so quiet and brooding lately. Did he seem off last weekend?" He wasn't fooled by her forced nonchalance.

"He seemed great," John said quickly, "his regular old self."

In actuality, Danny spent their hunting trip in near silence, glued to his phone and hardly eager to venture out of the cabin. But John couldn't tell Becca that, not when she was already so worried.

"Well, that's good, anyway," Becca replied half-heartedly. He didn't know how to make her believe him.

John glanced out the window again, this time scanning the entire parking lot. His son's white car was nowhere to be seen, and he'd notice if it were there, despite the ever-present cars of early morning tourists. Danny was probably the only one in twenty miles with tinted windows and they stuck out like a sore thumb. Waste of money in John's opinion, but who can tell young people anything?

"John? Are you still there?"

"Sorry - I'm here."

"Did you see the paper?"

"Yes, I saw the goddamned paper, Becca. Why is everyone so determined to keep reading and writing the same articles over and over?"

"Did you see the part at the bottom? The services offered?"

"No..." John's stomach dropped.

"It looks like... Well, it looks like they are throwing in a full mobile and online grocery suite. Order from your phone, pick up outside. They'll bring it right to the car."

John swore loudly.

"John! It's going to be fine. We'll figure something out..."

"No, Becca, I don't see how we will. I have to go." He hung up without waiting for a reply, then swore again in regret. She didn't deserve his anger, and he knew it.

John crossed the room in two steps and snatched the crumpled paper from the floor. He smoothed it out on his desk, scanning the print until he found the section Becca mentioned. An advertisement for the new supermarket sat beneath the article about Sue's expected approval of the retail complex.

Take Grocery Shopping Into This Century!

No more waiting around in lines, scrambling to carry your basket to the register, or searching endless shelves for what you need. Simply download our app, search, click, pay, and we'll bring it to you! Also available on your favorite web browser.

Coming to Cove Harbor next spring...

John grit his teeth. How was he supposed to keep up with this? Sure, he wasn't so old as to be a technology idiot, but this was beyond his capabilities for sure. An app?! Where do you even get one of those?

It was bad enough they would outprice him at every turn and likely have a better inventory. But what was he supposed to do? Everything had become so expensive. He needed to raise prices just to keep food on the table and make his ever-growing rent for the space on Main Street.

He looked down again at Sue's smile, frozen in black and white, one arm raised in a campaign-happy wave over a familiar background. The picture had been taken at the top of the hill in front of Cove Harbor High, their alma mater.

Maybe he could talk to her, John thought, picking his phone back up. They'd known each other for years. That had to count for something, right? He searched her name in his contacts, but nothing popped. Unsurprising, as he hadn't called her since she left for Boston after high school graduation.

Closing the app, he pulled up the Google search bar Bo recently added to his phone's home screen. Moments later, the mayor's office line rang in his ear.

An unfamiliar, airy female voice answered the phone.

"Mayor Clark's office, how can I help you?"

"Uh...Yes, hi," John began, unsure what to ask for. "I need to speak to Sue."

"And who is this?"

"John Scott."

"John....Scott...? Do you have a call scheduled?"

Annoyance flared in him.

"No, I don't have a call scheduled. We put her in that office; can't you just call and talk to her?"

"That's not how it's done, sir. What is this regarding?"

"Look, just tell her it's John Scott. We're old friends and I'd like to speak to her."

A small sigh followed before, "Please hold for a moment."

John waited, Cove Harbor High's school song playing in his ear. The little tune brought him back to baseball games and bus rides home with his team. He remembered school spirit days and bonfires, simplicity and easy times, though they didn't always feel so, then.

As he listened, John mulled over what to say to Sue. He would explain the situation, he thought, just be honest. Tell her the complex would destroy his and other small businesses. That it wasn't right. That maybe if she pulled her support from the project and withheld her approvals, they could stop the regional chain from invading their little village.

"Mr. Scott?"

"Yes, I'm here."

"I'm sorry, but Mayor Clark is unavailable."

"Unavailable? What the hell does that mean? Is she in

there or not!?"

"Excuse me..."

"You know what, forget it!" John smashed his finger into the little red button, lamenting the lost satisfaction of slamming a landline phone.

He let his cell drop to the desk, just inches from Sue's smiling face. It incited him, this oh-so-happy woman who was ruining his livelihood. And she didn't care. She didn't even have the decency to pick up his call.

John checked his watch. He could just walk right over to the Municipal Building and knock on her door. People rely too much on phones these days, anyway. She couldn't ignore him forever. He was an important part of this community. He and every other local business owner mattered, dammit.

Whatever it took, he'd make her hear what he had to say.

JANE ALLEN

July 26
11:25 AM

Snip, snip!

Jane's scissors sliced quietly to the beat of the salon's soft bossa nova. It was a quiet day, just Jane and her client reflected in the wall of Hollywood-lit mirrors. A solitary woman tapped her foot while her nails dried, one of the few who still came in for traditional polish. It was nostalgic, really.

Jane ignored the vibrations in her back pocket as she concentrated on the layers she added to Amy's waves. The younger woman's hair was nearly as dark as her own, although neither could claim the natural color, born as it was of careful hours in this very chair.

"You can pick that up if you want," Amy said, "I don't mind."

"It's all right," Jane replied, sliding her phone from her pocket and silencing the ring. "It's probably not important." Her voice faltered as she glanced at the caller ID. It was the station again.

Jane sighed as she placed it on the small counter with her collection of tools and sprays. She had a pretty good idea of why the police chief was calling and wanted to finish with Amy before handling it. Her problems weren't going anywhere, that was certain.

Jane concentrated on the neat layers, engaged by Amy's chit-chat and anticipation for the summer season: equal parts eagerness for beach weather and distaste for entitled tourists with a smattering of conversation about a summer art auction mixed in. The minutes ticked by on the pink plastic wall clock, a metronome keeping time until Amy's hair fell perfectly, effortlessly framing her heart-shaped face. Jane pocketed the tip, thanked Amy, and wished her a pleasant afternoon before stepping back from her station.

She leaned into the mirror, raising a finger to her sparkling purple eye shadow. Jane bit her lip, sliding a fingernail under her eye to wipe away an out-of-place smudge. It disappeared easily, helped along by the moisture of the hot July day. Even in the air-conditioned salon, they could feel the humidity hanging thickly around them.

"Your 12:00 is running late," came a shout from the front desk alcove. "She called a few minutes ago."

"Thanks, Bea."

Jane's phone clattered again, this time loud against the

counter. Sighing, Jane finally lifted it to her ear.

"Hello?"

"Hey, Jane. It's Bill."

It might be unusual for some chiefs of police to use a first name with a citizen, but this was Cove Harbor. They grew up on the same street, and Jane spent nearly every afternoon trudging through piles of homework in Bill's kitchen with his youngest sister. Jane had never addressed him as Chief Williams and probably never would.

"Let me guess - You're looking for Mark?"

"I'm sorry, Jane, you know I am," Bill hesitated. "But I think this is the end of the line for him. I can't hold off the others any longer. I need Mark to come in so we can have an official end to things."

"End to things? You mean he's fired?"

"Look, you know I did everything I could. But he's too often missing, and quite frankly, it's become dangerous when he is here. It's my ass on the line if something goes wrong because he's... Well, if you want to talk about a rehab program, maybe there's something I can do, but barring that..."

Jane pressed her fingers into her forehead.

"No, I understand. Thank you, Bill, for the call... for trying to cover for him... I'll see what we can do about a program and I'll let you know."

"Be well, Jane."

She disconnected the line. What were they going to do? They couldn't afford to live on her earnings from the salon, and things would only get more expensive as the twins got older. How would they pay for a rehab program? In all honesty, her husband probably needed one, but those programs were expensive, weren't they?

Jane dialed Mark's number, waiting, listening to the rings succumb to voicemail.

"Mark? Call me, please."

She dialed again, this time hanging up without leaving a message. And then once more, with a sinking heart and spark of frustration, before giving up.

Jane glanced at the clock. 11:50. She could find Mark after Vicky's appointment. She began collecting what she needed to touch up the young woman's pixie cut, keeping it choppy but not too harsh; blonde, but not platinum. The details made this more of an art than a day job.

Just as she finished setting up her station, her phone rang again. Distracted, she answered without checking the caller ID.

"Hello?"

"Jane? It's Colleen."

"Hey, Colleen. What can I do for you?" Jane already knew this couldn't be good. With a husband like hers, any call from a bartender at 11 am was bad news.

"I hate to call you like this, but I think you should come get Mark. He's in bad shape and needs to sleep it off."

"How urgent?" She glanced at the clock again. 11:58. "I'm at the salon."

"I'm sorry, Jane, but now would be best. He's been pretty

fired up and I'm not sure we can have him here much longer."

"Alright. I'll figure something out. Thanks for the call, Colleen."

"Anytime, Jane. Sorry again."

Jane returned her phone to her pocket and untied her smock, glancing around the salon. She hurried to the back room where Jackie held a fresh pot of coffee, ready to pour into her waiting mug. Hazelnut brew, Jane knew, even if she hadn't been able to smell it.

"Jackie? Can you cover my twelve o'clock? I have a little family emergency I need to take care of."

"Sure," Jackie replied, "I'm open until 2:15. Slow day, eh?"

"Thank you so much. I'll return the favor whenever you need."

"No biggie, really."

Not five minutes later, Jane hustled down the hot sidewalk towards Kelly's, one of the few remaining dives in the area and a local favorite. She pushed open the creaky door to the familiar smell of stale beer and ancient wood. A few linen-clad twenty-somethings chatted animatedly at the bar while Colleen wiped glasses behind the counter.

Looking up as Jane entered, Colleen nodded to the far corner where Mark was slumped in a booth, his hand inches from a tumbler of watery-looking liquor. His face, almost as red as his hair, shone with sweat as he hunched with sleep.

Jane approached Colleen first, a wary smile on her face.

"What happened?"

"Nothing too serious," Colleen replied, waving a hand, "just heckling a few of the other guys. And he smashed a glass. But the boss man will be back soon, and he won't hesitate to call the cops to remove him. I thought I'd give you the courtesy call, considering..."

"Thanks a million, really." Jane was relieved not to have to discuss this with Bill or see Mark embarrassed in front of the other officers.

How had they gotten here? Just a year ago, they'd been so happy. Playing with their little girls, living their regular, wonderfully boring lives. Sadness engulfed her as a small trickle of drool leaked from her husband's snoring mouth.

"Mark? Mark?" She shook his shoulder.

"What? Gettoffme," he mumbled, words strung together, tumbling clumsily over one another. She smacked him lightly on the cheek.

"Mark? It's Jane. Come on. It's time to leave."

"Jane?" He opened his eyes blearily. "How long was I asleep?"

"I don't know, Mark, but we need to go home." Thankfully, the nap seemed to have sobered him. He was still wasted, but at least he was talking and making eye contact.

"What happened?"

"Sounds like you made a bit of a scene before you passed out," Jane replied, annoyed that he didn't remember. "Colleen called me instead of the police."

"The police? I am the police! Ha. Ha. Ha."

"Not funny. Too soon." Jane replied.

How could she make him take this seriously? She knew she should wait for him to regain his senses before dropping the bomb, but something in his joking face wrestled the words right out of her.

"Mark, you're fired. Unless you go into rehab. Bill called."

"Fired?! I can't be fired. And I definitely don't need rehab."

"It's 11:30 in the morning and I'm getting calls from the bar to come get you! Why aren't you at work?! Why are you even here?!" Jane fought to control her temper, to restrain herself before she said something they couldn't come back from.

"I just stopped in for a minute on my way to work! Why is everyone on my case all the time?! Especially at the station, when they just blatantly ignore all the other fucked up shit going on in this town." He spat out the last sentence, moisture landing on the table between them.

"Oh, here we go, not this again..." Jane was tired of constantly having the same argument, dancing around Mark's feelings as her resentment for his baseless claims grew. "You lost the election Mark. I know it's been difficult for you to face, but you need to accept it and move on!"

"There's NO way I lost, Jane! I was going to win! It doesn't make any sense! That woman, she must've - "

"STOP, Mark! Just stop! Stop blaming everything on your crazy conspiracies! Sue Clark did not 'steal' your election! She didn't cheat; she just won. And your inability to get over it is the cause of all of these problems!"

He glared at her, his angry red flush a warning that she'd gone too far. But Jane had kept quiet for months and couldn't stop the words rushing out, couldn't control herself now that she'd started.

"What do you think, Sue Clark led you into the bar this morning?! Forced me to leave work?! Got you fired?! Made you embarrass me and your kids - God, your *kids*, what will the girls think of you? Enough is enough, Mark! You need a rehab program, and -"

"STOP, Jane!" Mark shot to his feet, reaching for the half-empty glass in front of him. To her disgust, he tipped the diluted drink into his mouth. "Let's go see her, then, Jane! Let's go!" He gestured wildly before slamming the glass back down, making her jump.

"See who? Sue Clark? You really will be arrested, Mark. Calm down!"

"She'll tell you, Jane! My wife, who doesn't believe in her own husband! Mayor Sue Clark will tell you *what she did*."

And he was off, out the door and up the sidewalk, dodging tourists and nearly running down the alleyway to Main Street and the Municipal Building. Jane chased him up the steps as he entered, wishing she at least forced a breath mint into him before leaving Kelly's.

Mark led her past a large glass case behind the security desk, three weapons securely locked inside. Their confinement was part of the new initiative to keep firearms accessible but out of law enforcement's hands. Jane initially thought the new arrangement was overkill, but couldn't help be grateful for it now that her husband barged through the foyer in a drunken rage.

The security station was empty, and they passed unmolested, Mark's eyes lingering on the gun case as they flew towards Mayor Clark's office. Her secretary's desk was as barren as the security station, and Jane sighed with relief, determined to talk Mark out of this confrontation.

She reached for Mark's arm as he strode towards the slightly ajar door, heavy and important with "Mayor" glinting on its nameplate.

"Please," Jane whispered, "Please, wait a minute. Think about what you're doing!"

Mark hesitated, his eyes on hers. She swore something softened there, but only momentarily, quickly hardening again with his resolve.

And then... a voice drifted through the door: Mayor Sue Clark, on the phone.

"I know you got me the election! I'm not stupid!" the mayor's voice was hushed and angry. "But I can't do it anymore! I'm not a liar, and I'm not a cheat. I need to come clean!"

Jane's eyes widened in shock.

"Hey! You there! What do you think you're doing!?"

A man in round glasses emerged from a door across the hall. Jane recognized him. He was the mayor's assistant. Boris? No, Benny. Yes, it was Benny.

Jane's fingers tightened on Mark's arm, just moments from pushing the door further open, seconds from attacking the mayor with his wild accusations. Although, clearly they weren't as wild as they seemed.

"Nothing! Sorry, we were just leaving." Jane gazed meaningfully into Mark's eyes, silently pleading with him to follow her. She finally knew the truth, and there could be no going back. But if they had any hope of fixing this, of a future, Mark needed to come with her now.

Because he'd been right about everything. Sue Clark stole the election from her husband, the good-hearted champion of the local people. She'd snatched it from him, left Mark only with the bitter disappointment and rage that poisoned him from within and destroyed their family.

Determination mingled with the reckless fury rising in her. As long as Mark left this horrible building with her, as long as he didn't cause this twitchy little man to call security, they could fix this. They would take their town back from Sue Clark, together.

And to Jane's immense relief, Mark lowered his arm, letting it fall loosely to his side as he followed her back to Main Street.

AMBER DAVIS

July 26
12:20 PM

A ferry plowed through the Hudson, its heavy wake trailing rivets through the greenish water. People congregated on the outdoor decks, sipping drinks and sharing snacks, work bags slung over their shoulders and littering the ground around their feet.

Far above, Amber Davis looked down on them, her upturned nose wrinkling at the idea of the river smell. It certainly wasn't her preferred method of travel.

"Amber? Are you listening?"

"Yes, Vlad, I'm *listening*." She pulled her eyes from the wide window, narrowing them at the tall man leaning against the designer couch, trailing his thin fingers over the shiny black leather she'd selected in honor of her last promotion. "I told you, the investments are secure. We are on schedule for two new complexes, one in Connecticut and one in Cove Harbor. Both are guaranteed profitable. Stop bothering me with your incessant follow-ups."

"I don't need to tell you what's at stake, Amber. A lot of money hangs in the balance. If we screw this up..."

Amber rolled her eyes and waved him away. He turned on his heel, agitated, but dismissed. She watched him disappear around the curve of her assistant's desk before she stalked across the room, heels clicking loudly against the hard floor. She pulled the glass door closed with a near-inaudible thud.

Thankful for the privacy coating on her office doors and windows, Amber sank into the chair behind her desk. She dangled one heel from her toe and gratefully rubbed her sore foot. Practical footwear was one of the few luxuries a woman like her couldn't afford. Not when her authority depended on an image of unbreakable ferocity and a nerve as sharp as the stilettos beneath her.

It irked her endlessly that Vlad was on her case about the new complexes. She hated being spoken to as if she didn't understand her role or their business plan. She was willing to bet Vlad wouldn't treat her like such a child if she'd been wearing Oxfords instead of Louboutins.

Vlad didn't like her in the top spot and hadn't hesitated to seize every opportunity to snake her position these past few years. But Amber was no fool. She'd clawed her way into this office, and she'd claw his eyes right out if he came for her job again.

Amber leaned forward, jabbing a button on her desk phone. It beeped, and a light flashed green.

"Gwen?"

"Yes, Ms. Davis?" her assistant's low voice crackled through the receiver.

"Could I have a coffee, please?"

"Sure, Ms. Davis. I'll get you one right away! Thank you!"

Amber's lips pressed together tightly, restraining her annoyance. She hated desperation, and Gwen personified it, willing to do anything for even just the possibility of a referral down the line. She was Amber's least favorite type of woman: Hungry for success but without the gumption to get out there and demand the respect she deserved.

Amber sat at her her laptop and selected a folder on the desktop, opening a collection of documents, PDF files, and spreadsheets. She double-clicked the spreadsheet at the top of the list, absently tapping her fingers on the cool glass desk as it lit up her monitor.

She bit her lip as she scrolled down the little boxes, checking a few numbers here and there. Everything would be fine with her investors. They were cutting things a little close, but her instincts and calculations agreed that Cove Harbor would be the key to their success.

The little tourist hub was a gold mine for a complex like the one she had planned. Locals would jump for their affordable goods as the cost of living continued to skyrocket, and tourists would ensure they make a fortune in the summer months, especially now that the grocery chain was perfecting mobile ordering.

She wasn't the first to attempt such a large retail space in the small town. But unlike her forebearers, Amber planned ahead. The Cove Harbor locals could be a hostile bunch, fighting every shade of big retail with all they had, but Amber was prepared. She had Sue Clark's support. And with it, there wouldn't be anything anyone could do to stop the construction. Those little community organizations didn't stand a chance.

Still... She'd better check in, just to make sure Sue's approvals would clear this week. Vlad would be giddy if the deal fell through, solidly affirming what he already believed – that Amber wasn't good enough to call the shots. If this didn't work out, she might as well pack up her desk and welcome Vlad inside to install his ugly bookshelves and hang his trashy art.

Amber picked up her phone and dialed the Cove Harbor mayor's office. The light female voice answered on the second ring.

"Mayor Clark's office, how can I help you?"

"Amber Davis for Sue Clark."

"Please hold a moment."

A twangy song erupted in her ear, and Amber pulled the phone away. How *annoying*. She'd have to tell Sue to replace it with something easier on the ears.

"Hello?"

"Hello, Mayor Clark. How are you?"

"Not great, Amber, to be honest. I was planning to call you

this afternoon."

Amber stopped scrolling down her spreadsheet.

"What's happened, Mayor Clark?"

The mayor did not reply. Amber listened as Sue Clark dismissed her assistant, requesting that he please step out to pick up their lunch, then fiddled with something rattling on her desk.

"Mayor Clark?" Amber didn't have all day to wait around for this woman.

"I can't do this anymore, Amber." She took a deep breath. "I'm out."

"Out?" Amber's voice was dangerously quiet. "Out of what?"

"Out of this! Out of all it! It's too much, and I don't want anything to do with it anymore."

The woman was raving, Amber thought. She closed her computer.

"You cannot be *out*, Mayor Clark. That is not how this works. I put you into that office, and I gave you your election. It's time to pay the piper."

"I know you got me the election! I'm not stupid!" the mayor's voice was hushed and angry. "But I can't do it anymore! I'm not a liar, and I'm not a cheat. I need to come clean!"

"Come clean?" Amber laughed out loud, but there was no humor there, no joy. "To whom, dear woman? Surely you will not risk your own position and your freedom over this bout of conscience..."

"The complex you want to build is asking too much. It's not right. It's bad for Cove Harbor." Sue Clark's voice was becoming stronger, and Amber's fury grew with Sue's conviction. "This is my home..."

"Mayor Clark. You will not jeopardize your position, the complex, or my business. Not in any way. You knew what you were getting into when you entered into our agreement. I held up my end and expect you to do the same."

Amber's words were as cold and calculating as she was. They had a deal, and that was that. There was nothing else to say to this stupid, small-town nobody.

"Amber, I'm out. I'm not approving the complex. Do whatever you want with my reputation. I'm coming clean this afternoon, and it will all be over."

"Sue - "

"Goodbye, Amber. And good riddance."

The phone clicked. The line went dead.

Amber slammed the receiver down, then picked it up and slammed it again.

Who did she think she was, this Sue Clark, ruining her plans? Reneging on their deal? Taking advantage of Amber's generosity and kindness? If it weren't for Amber, Clark would still be sucking up to the lowliest politicians in Boston, begging for their endorsements. The woman had some nerve.

Amber stood and took a deep breath, settling herself. This wasn't over. There had to be another way. There was *always* another way, always a contingency plan.

Her desk phone beeped, and Gwen's voice echoed through the speaker.

"Ms. Davis? I have your coffee."

Amber took one final moment to collect herself before pressing the button on her intercom.

"Bring it in, Gwen. Thanks."

Her assistant stepped into the room, hurrying over the stone flooring. Amber accepted the tall white cup, relishing the hot liquid as it poured down her throat, enlivening her.

"Anytime, of course. Thank you so much, Ms. Davis." Gwen's eager voice, always so annoying, sounded even more desperate than usual to Amber's frustrated ears. She frowned, and Gwen turned to leave.

An idea came to her as she watched her assistant leave the office, clomping away in her off-putting flats. She knew what she needed to do next. Amber slid open her bottom drawer and reached inside, slowly retrieving an unmarked black phone.

BENNY LEE

July 26
2:45 PM

Classical music emanated from a quiet speaker as Benny Lee scribbled furious circles across his notepad, leaving nothing but empty dents in the thin paper. He shook his pen violently, then cursed under his breath when it still failed to make a mark. He dropped it onto his desk and pushed back his chair, wheeling roughly over the worn carpet.

Benny strode across the stuffy room to a small crate of office supplies on the shelf near the wall heater. A window sat open above, but the air remained still and stifled by the July heat. Wiping sweat from his brow, Benny snagged a new pen from the box on top, one of the few black ones remaining in the mixed collection.

He knew he should unpack the supplies and fill his desk with the materials. Sue gave it all to him nearly a year ago now, just a few weeks after they won the election. But if he unpacked that one, he'd have to unpack the other one, too, and he didn't think he could handle that.

Returning to his seat, Benny pushed his glasses higher along the bridge of his nose and began his to-do list for the afternoon.

To Do

1. Confirm agenda for Harbor Bridge fundraising meeting

2. Return call to Cove Harbor High School guidance department re: internships

3. Prepare for Harbor Festival Planning Committee Meeting

4. Prepare agenda for morning town meeting

He examined the list for a moment before adding one more task to his list.

5. Call mom

Benny hadn't been in touch with his parents in a few weeks, not since Jenna's new relationship invaded his social media feeds. He knew his sister would've seen it too, and he didn't want to talk to her or his mother about the situation.

Without wanting or meaning to, Benny pulled out his

phone. His notifications included three missed calls from an unknown 917 number. Probably spam.

Ignoring the missed calls, he opened social media and typed Jenna's handle into the search bar. It's funny how even though you know it's bad for you, sometimes you just can't help seeking out your own worst triggers, the ones that hit you hard, right in the gut.

And there it was, Jenna's smiling face, leaning forward under the weight of the masculine arm draped over her shoulder. The guy looked broader than Benny, though probably not as tall. She looked happy. He should've blocked her.

He glanced up as his office phone beeped.

"Benny?" Sue's voice crackled over the intercom.

"What's up?"

"Do you happen to have a photo of our old team in Boston?"

"Maybe...Why?"

"Can you take a look and bring it to our three-clock check-in?"

"Um, sure." Benny glanced at his watch. 2:56.

"Thank you. See you in a few minutes."

Sighing, Benny strode over to the second box near the heater, the one he'd avoided for months. It was filled with the dusty decor of his little shoebox of an office back in Boston. He braced himself, then grit his teeth and pushed off the cover.

He removed an old photo of him and Jenna from the top

and placed it on the ground. There was his Red Sox bobblehead and a wrinkled green tie, piled haphazardly atop his old apartment keys and a stack of scribbled greeting cards. He picked up a small velvet box, heavy with rejection in his hand, and put it aside.

There, about halfway down, was a small black frame bursting with smiling faces. A note was taped to the front. *Best of luck in Cove Harbor! We'll miss you!* Benny tore off the faded paper and dropped it back in the box. He tucked his blue spiral notebook under his arm with the photograph and left for Sue's office.

"Hi, Benny," Sue greeted him as he knocked on the open door. She looked worn and tired, nothing like the vibrant woman she'd been in those early months after the election. He sat in one of the chairs facing her desk and opened his notebook to the items they needed to discuss this afternoon. She held up a hand.

"Wait, please. We need to talk."

"Okay..." Benny had no idea what was coming.

"Do you have that photograph I asked you to bring?" He laid it on the desk in front of her. His phone vibrated just as he was about to ask why she needed it.

"Sorry," Benny said quickly, pulling it out. It was that same 917 number. He ignored the call.

"No problem, Benny." Sue picked up a photo on her desk and showed it to him. In it, Sue smiled broadly beside a young woman with shoulder-length blonde hair. She stood proudly, holding a framed certificate up for the camera.

"This is my niece, Alexis. My sister Kate's daughter. Alexis is attending college in the fall to study political science. She wants to work in local government, just like me, to make a positive difference in people's lives."

Benny nodded, unsure what to say. Sue set down the photograph.

"Do you know Scott's Grocery?"

Benny nodded again, still confused. "Yes. I live across the street, as you know, so I get most of my groceries there." Sure, the store was a little overpriced, but you couldn't beat its convenience when you lived and worked on Main Street.

"Well, John Scott's family has owned that store for three generations. It's a true local business. And he came to see me this afternoon. He's afraid they will go under when the new complex is built."

Benny was starting to see where this might be heading, and he didn't want to hear it.

"Sue, are you saying what I think you're - "

"Please, let me finish."

"Fine..." Benny replied uneasily, fidgeting in his seat.

"When I started on the path to politics, I wanted to help people. I came back to Cove Harbor to make a difference in the lives of the people I grew up alongside and care about. I couldn't do that in Boston because the people I love, generally, are here."

Benny flushed. He'd left everyone in his life behind for this boring town, and they'd all moved on without him back home. His friends, Jenna... Nobody even bothered to text him anymore. But Benny remained silent, waiting for the mayor to finish before he spoke.

Sue again picked up the photo of her niece.

"When I look at this photo, I see my niece, inspired by me to do good. But am I doing good anymore? I see a young woman, full of promise, and an older one who's forgotten what's truly important. That's what I see. And I hate it."

Sue set down the photo of her niece and raised the one of their team in Boston. Benny was feeling extremely uncomfortable now and more than prickled by her words. When he followed Sue home to where her heart was, he'd been forced to give up his own. He thought of that stupid velvet box back in his office.

"When you look at this photo, what do you see?"

"I see our old team."

"What do you really see, Benny? What did you want back then? What do you want now? Would the you in this photo be proud of who you've become?"

"I see *me*! I wanted to be successful back then and still want to be successful now! That's why I came here with you, right? To be your right hand while you are the mayor? To run for my own office in the next election?"

She cleared her throat and looked away from his intense gaze.

"Sue, what are you trying to tell me?" His glasses slid down his nose and he shoved them back up. "Out with it."

"I can't do it anymore, Benny. I called Amber today and told her the deal is off."

"The deal is off? The deal cannot *be* off, Sue! I don't think it works like that."

"I told her it was, Benny. It's over. I need you to call a press conference today so I can make a public statement. It's time to come clean."

"Like hell, I'll call a press conference! I'm not doing it, Sue, no way! This is not only your decision to make! What about me?! I gave up *everything* for this! For you!"

"I know, Benny. I understand how hard this is for you."

"No, you don't!" Benny was seething. Sue had no idea what he'd given up. She'd never bothered to ask him about his life. No, it was always 'how do we get Sue into office,' or 'how do we make sure Sue gets what she wants?' He'd given up so much, *everything*, and now...

"Benny, please try to understand. We never should have listened to Amber Davis. We should have done it the right way! If we ran fair and square, we might still have beaten Mark Allen."

He stood and picked up his notebook.

"Yeah, right, Sue. I'm not calling that press conference. And you sure as shit shouldn't either." Benny needed space. He needed to clear his head.

"Benny - "

"Keep that stupid photograph," he said angrily, "I don't need it." And with that, he stalked out of her office. He crossed the threshold of his own and stopped short, anger pulsing through him.

Benny wound up and hurled his notebook at the far wall,

where it smacked into the cracked plaster and fell to the ground. Damn, that felt good. He flung the pen after it. Then he walked to the box brimming with ghosts of his old life and kicked it, satisfaction erupting when something inside shattered.

He glanced outside, breathing heavily as his eyes fell on his apartment window. There was nothing there but ugly blinds, their cheap metal grimy after nearly a year without cleaning. Benny hadn't bothered to hang curtains or decorate and hardly ever cleaned.

What was the point? Nobody ever visited.

His phone vibrated again in his pocket. The same unknown number that had been calling him all day flashed across the screen as he withdrew it. Benny swore under his breath, but finally pressed the little green button to take the call.

MAYOR, MURDERED

July 26
3:45 PM

The late afternoon sun beat down on the crowd. Mark Allen stood in silence, a dull hangover throbbing behind his ears. His earlier anger with his wife had evaporated as she finally accepted the truth, finally understood, returning to her place by his side. He watched her across the crowd, bright eyes glued on the podium where Mayor Clark would soon appear.

He couldn't stop looking at her, her curvy figure standing out amongst the wiry frames of two women behind her. She was like a pin-up girl, his Jane, with her dark hair and beautiful face. Mark didn't know how he got so lucky.

He knew he'd messed up big time. Worse than ever before. But he also had hope now, and he believed everything would be alright. Jane always knew what to do, and they could move past this dark time together. He could get his life in order.

Mark reached into his inside pocket and felt the cold steel of the flask there. He touched it but didn't pull it out. He didn't even want it. Mark smiled nervously at his wife, hoping she'd give him the chance to get out of the doghouse permanently, but she didn't notice him.

Behind her, a car engine rumbled, though it remained motionless in a parking spot. The tinted windows prevented the crowd from seeing the young man sitting inside with his father, concern on both their faces.

"I don't like you not showing up to work, Danny. Your mother and I were worried."

"I'm not a little kid anymore, Dad."

"I know that, but you're also my employee. You need to be at the store when you're scheduled to be there. Bo covered for you today, but that's not right either - He needs to finish summer school to get his diploma."

"I know, Dad, really. I'm sorry."

"It's alright, Danny." John looked his son directly in the eye. "Now, tell me where you were. Enough of this sneaking around, moping in the cabin, never giving us a straight answer about what you're doing. What's going on with you?"

"I was hoping to wait to tell you this until I knew it would work, but..." his son trailed off.

"What is it?" The worry ebbed from John as excitement expanded across his son's features.

"I've been working with a buddy of mine - Abe, you know,

from the college? - And he's helping me set up an app for the store." Danny whipped out his phone and turned it toward his father. "Check this out!"

"Danny!" John couldn't believe his eyes as the store's logo flashed in front of him, fading to images of grocery items.

"Look Dad, see, you can browse, and order, and..."

John watched his son tapping around the little screen, and a liberating realization spread through him. He wasn't in this alone. He had never been. Not really. Scott's Grocery belonged to all the Scotts, and together, they would keep it alive.

Just as John had added his own expertise to the knowledge of the generations before him, Danny's was the promise of the future. John felt the emotion spreading through his chest, filling his throat, finally prickling behind his eyes. He rested his hand on his son's arm and leaned in closer for the tutorial.

While Danny was reminding John of the true heart and soul of a family business, Mayor Sue Clark sat alone at her desk, staring intently at the photo of her niece.

Her mind raced with worry and fear. She never meant for any of this to happen. She didn't know exactly when her integrity had gone out the window, but somewhere along the line, it had, and it was time to reel it back in.

John Scott reminded her today of what she'd already begun to realize. She was a changed person, and not for the better. She loved this little town more than anything, but in loving it, she'd sold its soul to the devil.

She could've been a great mayor. She still believed that. But she should've played fair in the last election. She should've spat in Amber Davis' face the moment she approached her in that coffee shop in Boston.

But she'd been foolish and hungry for power, ever tired of living and working in a city that didn't love her. She wanted to come home and work for the local people of Cove Harbor, to protect those who'd meant so much to her over the years.

Amber gave her an opportunity to do that, and she took it - Sold out for the top job. Mark Allen never stood a chance, though he'd never understood why. How could he have known? Who would've expected it from her? Not Sue Clark, the ambitious and celebrated student council president of Cove Harbor High.

Sue looked into the static eyes of her niece, as similar to hers as her own child's might have been. She thought of the disappointment and shame that would cloud Alexis' face when she learned of Sue's crimes and of every opportunity for a family of her own that she'd given up for her career. It was all for nothing, now.

Regardless, she had to come clean. Sue needed to set an example for Alexis and all the other young women out there. She'd made a mistake, but she would own up to it and face the consequences. She wouldn't let her own faults become those of future generations. They could learn from her.

With a deep breath, Sue gathered her notes and rose from her desk. She turned for one last look at her office before making her way down to the podium. She would return a disgraced politician, not a promising new mayor. What she was about to do would change everything, forever.

Sue glanced at Benny's closed office door as she passed. He was so angry with her. She could hear his music but supposed he wouldn't join her at the press conference. His unwavering support had finally faltered. So be it, she thought sadly. One day he would understand. One day, he would forgive her.

She walked slowly down the hall, knowing she was a few minutes late but unable to force herself to move faster. Her eyes lingered on the glass security case along the hallway. Something seemed off, but everything felt strange right now. She didn't look back.

Sue emerged from the building, squinting in the sunlight, and took her place behind the podium. She tapped the microphone and heard the vibration reverberate through the crowd.

Finally, she spoke.

"Welcome, everyone. Thank you for joining me today on such short notice."

She needed to keep talking but couldn't force the words out. She thought again of Benny, her poor assistant, and glanced up at his apartment across the street. To her surprise, Benny stood in the window, peering through the blinds as they moved slightly in the breeze. She met his eyes, startled. What was he doing up there? He looked at her, a pleading expression crossing his face.

No matter. He wasn't happy, but this needed to be done. She would try to spare him as much of the fallout as possible. She took a deep breath. It was time to confess.

"I called you all here today to tell you something difficult but important. I - "

Crack!

A shot rang out, followed by two more in quick succession. Mayor Sue Clark's eyes widened in shock as blood blossomed across her chest. She crumpled, dead before she hit the ground, and chaos erupted around her.

High above the street, the barrel of a gun lowered from behind the dirty blinds of an open window. Benny Lee moved quickly, taking apart the pieces and placing them into the inside pockets of his coat.

He would sneak down the back staircase of his building and return the gun to their office security box while everyone was distracted by the mayor's death. Then, he would emerge from the Municipal Building, feigning shock and concern at the commotion.

Nobody would know. And even if they did, he had people to protect him now.

But first, he needed to make a call.

He retrieved the convenience store burner he'd purchased less than an hour earlier and held down the redial button. It rang twice before Amber Davis' voice answered.

"Hello?"

"It's done."

"Wonderful, Mr. Lee. Or should I say, Mr. Mayor."

ACKNOWLEDGMENTS

First and foremost, thank you to my husband, Jeff Dunworth, a.k.a. the 'Idea Guy,' without whom this mystery collection would not exist in any tangible form. I can't thank you enough for your endless companionship, support, and hours driving around talking through every plot of my stories, making them better together.

Thank you to my kids, James, Ellie Jo, and Sophie, for being the best reasons to get up in the morning and the driving force behind everything I do.

Thank you to my parents: To my mother, Janet Verneuille, for instilling in me a love of reading that has been a pillar of my life for as long as I can remember and for teaching me how to write. To my father, Tom Verneuille, for teaching me how to take what is in front of me, see it for what it is, and turn it into something better. And for the grit.

Thank you to my sister, Emily Verneuille, for helping me understand what it's like to play in a community band and for inspiring A Memorial Day Murder. Thank you to Lindsey D'Amato, and all the other teachers I've worked with over the years, for your jokes and experiences that made it into Murder in the Main Office.

Thank you to all my wonderful friends and family who are always willing to read a draft, provide feedback, check formatting, and help with anything I've ever asked for. A special shout out to Kelly Palmese, Liz Forester, Mary

Callaghan, and Jen Callaghan Kash for your feedback on these mysteries, and another for Jeremy Goldstein, a fellow author, for the camaraderie across professions and for being a helpful set of eyes on this short story collection. I'm so lucky to have all of you in my corner.

Thank you to my brother Ryan Verneuille and to everyone who has supported me in writing this and everything else I've accomplished over the years.

And thank you to all of you for reading it now.

Finally, thank you to my hometown for inspiring these mysteries and providing me with the foundations of love and friendship that have always made everything else in my life possible. Without you, I could never have been me.

ABOUT THE AUTHOR

Anna Dunworth is a history teacher turned author who writes mysteries, short fiction, and young adult fantasy.

Seeking a balance between the comfortable familiarity of the human spirit and the next best edge-of-your-seat twist, her work incorporates meaningful themes into lighthearted stories inspired by life's overlooked corners.

Anna received her BA in Communication and History from SUNY Geneseo and her Masters in Teaching Social Studies from Stony Brook University. She currently lives along the Connecticut shoreline with her family.

Read more of Anna's work at **www.annadunworth.com**.

www.ingramcontent.com/pod-product-compliance
Lightning Source LLC
Chambersburg PA
CBHW020132120726
47903CB00007B/2218